THE OPPOSITE OF

LONELINESS

THE OPPOSITE OF LONELINESS

Essays and Stories

MARINA KEEGAN

**SIMON &
SCHUSTER**

London · New York · Sydney · Toronto · New Delhi

A CBS COMPANY

First published in Great Britain by Simon & Schuster UK Ltd, 2014
This paperback edition published by Simon & Schuster UK Ltd, 2015
A CBS COMPANY

1 3 5 7 9 10 8 6 4 2

Simon & Schuster UK Ltd
1st Floor
222 Gray's Inn Road
London WC1X 8HB

www.simonandschuster.co.uk

Simon & Schuster Australia, Sydney
Simon & Schuster India, New Delhi

A CIP catalogue record for this book
is available from the British Library

Jacket design by Janet Hansen
Jacket photograph © Joy Shan

Paperback ISBN: 978-1-47113-962-8
eBook ISBN: 978-1-47113-963-5

The author and publishers have made all reasonable efforts
to contact copyright-holders for permission, and apologise
for any omissions or errors in the form of credits given.
Corrections may be made to future printings.

Printed and bound by CPI Group (UK) Ltd, Croydon, CR0 4YY

Dedication

"I will live for love and the rest will take care of itself" were Marina's words on graduation day, the last time we saw her. *The Opposite of Loneliness* is dedicated to love. Our hope is that Marina's message of love will inspire readers to imagine the possibilities and make a difference in the world.

Tracy and Kevin Keegan

Do you wanna leave soon?
No, I want enough time to be in love with everything . . .
And I cry because everything is so beautiful and so short.

—Marina Keegan, from the poem "Bygones"

Contents

NONFICTION

Introduction

I first saw Marina Keegan on November 10, 2010. I was hosting the novelist Mark Helprin at a master's tea at Yale, during which he said that making it as a writer today was virtually impossible.

A student stood up. Thin. Beautiful. Long, reddish-brown hair. Long legs. Flagrantly short skirt. Nimbus of angry energy. She asked Helprin if he really meant that. There was a collective intake of breath in the room. It was what everyone else had been thinking but no one else had been brave (or brazen) enough to say.

That night, I got an e-mail from marina.keegan@yale.edu:

> Hello! I don't think you know me, but I was the student who asked the question . . . Hearing a famous writer tell me that the industry is dying and that we should probably do something else was sad. Perhaps I just expected him to be more encouraging of those hoping to *stop* the death of literature.

"To stop the death of literature": Marina was being simultaneously self-mocking (if she'd said that line aloud, she would have overacted, with plenty of pregnant pauses and overenunciated consonants, so you'd know it was hyperbole) and 100 percent serious.

She applied to my class on first-person writing a few weeks later. Her application began:

> About three years ago, I started a list. It began in a marbled notebook but has since evolved inside the walls of my word processor. *Interesting stuff.* That's what I call it. I'll admit it's become a bit of an addiction. I add to it in class, in the library, before bed, and on trains. It has everything from descriptions of a waiter's hand gestures, to my cab driver's eyes, to strange things that happen to me or a way to phrase something. I have 32 single-spaced pages of interesting stuff in my life.

In my class, which she took in the spring of her junior year, she drew on those thirty-two pages of interesting stuff to write a series of essays that her classmates, in their written critiques, festooned with awestruck adjectives: *beautiful, vivid, vibrant, visual, fresh, direct, lyrical, compelling, evocative, precise, confident, honest, startling.* (Three of the pieces in this book are from that class. Others are from Yale writing classes taught by John Crowley and Cathy Shufro; some are from student periodicals; and three—"Baggage Claim," "Sclerotherapy," and "I Kill for Money"—were written during Marina's junior and senior years at the Buckingham Browne & Nichols School, in classes taught by Harry Thomas and Brian Staveley.)

Many of my students sound forty years old. They are articulate but derivative, their own voices muffled by their desire to skip over their current age and experience, which they fear trivial, and land on some version of polished adulthood without passing Go. Marina was twenty-one and sounded twenty-one: a brainy twenty-one, a twenty-one who knew her way around the English language, a twenty-one who understood that there were few better subjects than being young and uncertain and starry-eyed and frustrated and hopeful. When she read her work aloud around our seminar table, it would make us snort with laughter, and then it would turn on a dime and break our hearts.

I always ask my students to append to their final essay a list of "Personal Pitfalls"—the aspects of their writing they wish to work on in the future. These were some of Marina's:

- Too much polysyndeton.* Watch it!
- Don't overdo the anaphora.**
- Be careful of weird strange phrases and their prepositions.
- Be careful of parallels.
- Make your titles good! Don't just choose them at the last minute! Avoid alliteration!
- Make sure modifiers make sense.
- Add more real stories when talking about general ideas.
- Make sure to spell-check homophones like "it's" and "its" by searching the document before finishing.
- Don't use too many adverbs in one sentence.
- Similes must actually be capable of doing their thing. You can't "curl up like a spoon."
- Unusual phrases work better at the end of paragraphs.
- I lay an egg, I laid an egg, I have laid an egg. I lie, I lay, I have lain.
- Topic indecision—just get over it!
- Make sure tenses are consistent.
- Don't use two prepositions in a row.
- Don't get too attached to things. It only took you a minute to write that sentence!
- THERE CAN ALWAYS BE A BETTER THING!

---

* Polysyndeton is the use of multiple conjunctions: "A and B and C" instead of "A, B, and C."
** Anaphora is the repetition of initial words or phrases.

*   *   *

High on their posthumous pedestals, the dead become hard to see. Grief, deference, and the homogenizing effects of adulation blur the details, flatten the bumps, sand off the sharp corners. Marina was brilliant, kind, and idealistic; I hope I never forget that she was also fierce, edgy, and provocative. A little wild. More than a little contrarian. If you wanted a smooth ride, Marina wasn't your vehicle. When we met for an hour-long conference to edit her first essay together, we got through three and a half lines. She resisted my suggestions because she didn't want to sound like me; she wanted to sound like herself. In class, she had strong opinions about the writers we read. She hated Lucy Grealy even though most of her classmates loved her, and loved Joyce Maynard even though most of her classmates hated her. She both admired and envied other talented young writers. When I posted exemplary essays by two students from a previous class, she wrote, "AHHHH ALICE'S ESSAY IS SO GOOD OH MY GOD . . . . ELISA'S IS SO GOOD TOO! oh my gosh. No i won't get dampened . . ." She frequently lost her keys and her cell phone, sometimes for days, sometimes *inside* her bag, an infinitely capacious, ink-stained tote (you might have expected someone as entropic as Marina to choose a bag with a zipper, but, as in all else, openness was her hallmark); she was given to procrastination and the all-nighters that inevitably followed; she was frustrated by deadlines, bureaucracies, obtuse politicians, the gap between theory and practice, her roommates' habit of using a knife to cut bread and then dipping it in the Nutella jar, and her own tendency to forget things, all of which inspired the all-purpose e-mail-and-text expletive "GAH!"

The summer between her junior and senior years, everything went so well for Marina that she had few occasions to say GAH. She had once papered her bedroom wall with *New Yorker* covers; now she was interning in the *New Yorker*'s fiction department, combing its slush pile for hidden gems, and getting published on its book blog. One of her plays was selected for a staged reading at a major theater festival, and she wrote much of another by, as she put it, "clocking in 3 hours (no excuses) every day."

During that summer Marina also found time to write to her friends and teachers. Having just read an essay in which I'd mentioned the excuses that the poet Samuel Taylor Coleridge, an inveterate procrastinator, had made for his tardy correspondence, she began one e-mail:

I'm so sorry about the delay in writing to you! The fact of the matter is I've taken ill after wearing excessively thin breeches in bad weather—not to mention because of my toothache, insomnia, gout, cough, boils, inflamed eyes, swollen testicles, and raging epistolophobia.

And ended it:

And above all, be at peace with yourself, and a double Blessing to me, who am, my dear Professor, anxiously,

Your fond Student

(She explained in a postscript to a later e-mail: "Since reading those Coleridge letters I've become obsessed with these types of signatures. They're just so GOOD. Like, that moment with the comma before the line break. I love that moment. COLERIDGE! Thank you.")

But she couldn't wait to get back to college:

I'm realizing how much I love Yale. With my minutes before sleep preoccupied with The Future for the first time in a while, I'm beginning to regard Yale with a kind of premature nostalgia. I WANT TO TAKE EVERY CLASS IN THE CATALOGUE. I WANT TO SEE EVERY BUILDING. I WANT TO SPEND TIME WITH ALL MY FRIENDS.

And she did, pretty much, flying through her senior year with every pore open, collecting prizes, working as Harold Bloom's research assistant, acting in two plays and writing a third, serving as president of the Yale College Democrats, helping to organize Occupy Yale, taking the train to New York every Thursday to intern at the *Paris Review,* lining up a postgraduation job at the *New Yorker,* writing during every spare minute, falling in love. When a friend who had graduated the previous year asked her permission to show some of her work to his students in Peru, she responded, "Yes to everything!"

* * *

Five days after Marina graduated magna cum laude, I got an e-mail from another student of mine:

Anne, sorry to bother you this late, but there's some terrible news that I don't know if you've heard—please call me.

Marina's boyfriend had been driving her from brunch with her grandmother near Boston to her family's summer house on Cape Cod to celebrate her father's fifty-fifth birthday. Her parents were waiting with lobsters and, because Marina had Celiac Disease and couldn't digest wheat, a homemade gluten-free strawberry shortcake. Her boyfriend, who was neither speeding nor drinking, fell asleep at the wheel. The car hit a guardrail and rolled over twice. Marina was killed. Her boyfriend was unhurt.

Marina's parents invited him to their house the next day and embraced him. They wrote the state police to ask that no charges of vehicular homicide be brought because "it would break [Marina's] heart to know her boyfriend would have to suffer more than he already is." When he went to court, the Keegans accompanied him. The charges were dropped.

At Marina's memorial service, I had never seen so many young people cry—not just cry, but shake so hard I feared their ribs would break.

Within a week, "The Opposite of Loneliness," an essay that had appeared in the graduation issue of the *Yale Daily News,* had been read by more than a million people. "We're so young. *We're so young,*" Marina had written. "We're twenty-two years old. We have so much time."

When a young person dies, much of the tragedy lies in her promise: what she *would* have done. But Marina left what she had *already* done: an entire body of writing, far more than could fit between these covers. As her parents and friends and I gathered her work, trying to find the most recent version of every story and essay, we knew that none of it was in exactly the form she would have wanted to publish. She was a demon reviser, rewriting and rewriting and rewriting even when everyone else thought something was done. (THERE CAN ALWAYS BE A BETTER THING.) We knew we couldn't rewrite her work; only she could have done that. Still, every time I reread these nine stories and nine essays, they sound exactly like her, and I don't want to change a word.

Marina wouldn't want to be remembered because she's dead. She would want to be remembered because she's good.

* * *

I have seen too many young writers give up because they couldn't handle the repeated failures their profession threw at them. They had talent, but they lacked determination and resilience. Marina had all three, and that's why I am certain she would have succeeded.

She once wrote me on the night that Yale's secret societies—senior social clubs, including Skull and Bones, Scroll and Key, and Book and Snake, that meet in windowless buildings called tombs—tapped their new members. She had not been chosen. "I'm in our WaO room right now actually," she began. ("WaO" was the acronym for our writing class, Writing about Oneself. Marina joked that the following year its students should continue to meet for DaO, Drinking about Oneself.)

> I ended up getting a bit screwed over on the secret society front so I've vowed to spend the 12 hours a week writing a novel. (Tonight is tap.) If I was willing to devote that much time chatting in a tomb I should be willing to devote it to writing! 6–12 sundays and thursdays. Might call it BOOK and BOOK. :)

She had devoted less than two hours to disappointment before she moved on. If she'd been tapped by Book and Snake, this book would not exist.

After Marina's death, her father told me about a sailing race she'd entered when she was fourteen. The race—in Wellfleet Harbor, on the outer end of Cape Cod—was for a class of solo fourteen-foot dinghies called Lasers. The junior sailors, fifteen and under, were to start at the same time as the adults. Marina was hoping for a calm day. She thought she could beat everyone, including the adults, both because she was an expert sailor and because she weighed less than a hundred pounds. A heavy sailor slows a boat just as a heavy jockey slows a racehorse.

But the day wasn't calm. There were forty-knot winds and three-foot waves. Before the race started, the entire junior division dropped out, along with all the women—except Marina.

In weather like that, lightness is not an asset. Especially when the boat is heading upwind, keeping it stable is almost impossible. Marina capsized more times than her parents could count. Each time, the boat tipped onto its side and she was thrown into the water. She had to swim the bow into the wind, climb onto the centerboard, stand on it while holding onto the gunwale, lean backward, pull hard enough to lift seventy-six square feet of wet sail out of the water, climb back into the boat, and readjust the sail, all with the wind howling and the waves crashing into and over her.

Marina's original goal had been to win. Her new goal was to finish. Several of the men gave up, but Marina continued. In perfect weather, the race would have taken her fifteen minutes. It took her almost an hour. She came in second to last, to incredulous applause. She was soaking wet, her hair was bedraggled, and her hands were bloody from gripping the lines.

* * *

A few hours after Marina was told that making it as a writer today was virtually impossible, she arrived late to a meeting of her spoken-word poetry group at Yale. A friend of hers recalls that her face was flushed and her eyes were like sharp, wet stones.

"I've decided I'm going to be a writer," she said. "Like, a real one. With my life."

—Anne Fadiman
November 12, 2013

Acknowledgments

The Opposite of Loneliness would not have been possible without the assiduous efforts of Anne Fadiman, professor, mentor, and friend to Marina during her time at Yale. Anne has invested countless hours working tirelessly to make our dream of sharing Marina's work a reality. Anne's generosity of spirit is matched only by her brilliance. No words could adequately express the depth of our gratitude.

At Buckingham Browne & Nichols, Marina studied with Beth McNamara, a gifted teacher of English and kindred spirit. Ms. Mac's tutelage and encouragement were instrumental to Marina's development as a writer. We have come to treasure the bond formed with Beth as she has provided steadfast support to our family and expert editorial assistance on the book.

Our grateful recognition goes to literary agents Lane Zachary and Todd Shuster, who helped us to find the perfect publisher for Marina's work and we deeply appreciate the outstanding team at Scribner: Nan Graham, Shannon Welch, John Glynn, Kate Lloyd, Roz Lippel, Caitlin Dohrenwend, Kara Watson, Dan Cuddy, and Tal Goretsky. Marina would have been so honored.

Much of the vital collecting, organizing, and formatting of Marina's portfolio has been contributed by Vivian Yee, a friend and fellow English major. We are grateful for the hours of hard work and loving dedication she has contributed to the project.

Marina's dear friends Chloe Sarbib, Luke Vargas, and Yena Lee have constantly been there for us, helping to keep her spirit close and serving as trusted guides along the journey.

It is easy to understand the inspiration for Marina's final essay, as we have been embraced by Yale's amazing community of classmates, professors, and staff. We offer heartfelt thanks to the entire Yale community, and special mention must go to Harold Bloom, John Crowley, Paul Hudak, Amy Hungerford, Deborah Margolin, Donald Margulies, Paul McKinley, Mary Miller, Catherine Nicholson, Cathy Shufro, and Leslie Woodard.

The following people have contributed to Marina's legacy in a multitude of ways: Will Adams, Monrud Becker, Debby Bisno, Michael Blume, Luke Bradford, Joseph Breen, Alexandra Brodsky, Alex Caron, Wendy and Bill Coke, Carrie Cook, Gabriel Barcia Duran, Olivia Fragale, Stephen Feigenbaum, Jacque Feldman, Cory Finley, Riley Scripps Ford, Adam Freedman, Michael Gocksch, Henry Gottfried, Josh Grossman, Steve Grossman, Jack Hitt, Rachel Hunter, Cam Keady, Duke and Kathy Keegan, Tom and Lori Keegan, Michael and Luette Keegan, Shellie Keegan, Beatrice Kelsey-Watts, Zara Kessler, Julia Lemle, Dan Lombardo, Kate Lund, Richard Miron, David Mogilner, Lauren Motzkin, Nick Murphy, John-Michael Parker, Charlie Polinger, Michael Rosen, Rachel Ruskin, Kate Selker, Julie Shain, Raphael Shapiro, Diana Shoolman, Vivian Shoolman, Mark Sonnenblick, Ben Stango, Kathy and Jeff Starcher, Jim Stone, Eric Schwartz, Brendan Ternus, Jesse Terry, Gerrit Thurston, Sally Vargas, Sigrid von Wendel, Meghan Weiler, Ben Wexler, Joseph Wynant, Yael Zinkow, and Julie Zhu. Apologies to anyone we have inadvertently left out: You were certainly never left out of her heart.

In addition to her beloved Yale, Marina experienced the

opposite of loneliness in two other formative places: the Buckingham Browne & Nichols School and Cape Cod Sea Camp, where she spent her childhood summers.

In honor of Marina's brothers, Trevor and Pierce, with whom she shared a childhood full of spirit and adventure and for whom she had profound admiration and love.

Finally, we acknowledge our entire community of family and friends who have contributed to make this book a reality. It was comforting to have you there for us and we are grateful to have you in our lives.

Tracy and Kevin Keegan

THE OPPOSITE OF LONELINESS

The Opposite of Loneliness

We don't have a word for the opposite of loneliness, but if we did, I could say that's what I want in life. What I'm grateful and thankful to have found at Yale, and what I'm scared of losing when we wake up tomorrow after Commencement and leave this place.

It's not quite love and it's not quite community; it's just this feeling that there are people, an abundance of people, who are in this together. Who are on your team. When the check is paid and you stay at the table. When it's four A.M. and no one goes to bed. That night with the guitar. That night we can't remember. That time we did, we went, we saw, we laughed, we felt. The hats.

Yale is full of tiny circles we pull around ourselves. A cappella groups, sports teams, houses, societies, clubs. These tiny groups that make us feel loved and safe and part of something even on our loneliest nights when we stumble home to our computers—partnerless, tired, awake. We won't have those next year. We won't live on the same block as all our friends. We won't have a bunch of group texts.

This scares me. More than finding the right job or city or spouse, I'm scared of losing this web we're in. This elusive, indefinable, opposite of loneliness. This feeling I feel right now.

But let us get one thing straight: the best years of our lives are not behind us. They're part of us and they are set for repetition as we grow up and move to New York and away from New York and wish we did or didn't live in New York. I plan on having parties when I'm thirty. I plan on having fun when I'm old. Any notion of THE BEST years comes from clichéd "should have . . . ," "if I'd . . . ," "wish I'd . . ."

Of course, there are things we wish we'd done: our readings, that boy across the hall. We're our own hardest critics and it's easy to let ourselves down. Sleeping too late. Procrastinating. Cutting corners. More than once I've looked back on my high school self and thought: how did I do that? How did I work so hard? Our private insecurities follow us and will always follow us.

But the thing is, we're all like that. Nobody wakes up when they want to. Nobody did all of their reading (except maybe the crazy people who win the prizes . . .). We have these impossibly high standards and we'll probably never live up to our perfect fantasies of our future selves. But I feel like that's okay.

We're so young. *We're so young.* We're twenty-two years old. We have so much time. There's this sentiment I sometimes sense, creeping in our collective conscious as we lie alone after a party, or pack up our books when we give in and go out— that it is somehow too late. That others are somehow ahead. More accomplished, more specialized. More on the path to somehow saving the world, somehow creating or inventing or improving. That it's too late now to BEGIN a beginning and we must settle for continuance, for commencement.

When we came to Yale, there was this sense of possibility. This immense and indefinable potential energy—and it's easy to feel like that's slipped away. We never had to choose and suddenly we've had to. Some of us have focused ourselves.

Some of us know exactly what we want and are on the path to get it: already going to med school, working at the perfect NGO, doing research. To you I say both congratulations and you suck.

For most of us, however, we're somewhat lost in this sea of liberal arts. Not quite sure what road we're on and whether we should have taken it. If only I had majored in biology . . . if only I'd gotten involved in journalism as a freshman . . . if only I'd thought to apply for this or for that . . .

What we have to remember is that we can still do anything. We can change our minds. We can start over. Get a post-bac or try writing for the first time. The notion that it's too late to do anything is comical. It's hilarious. We're graduating from college. We're so young. We can't, we MUST not lose this sense of possibility because in the end, it's all we have.

In the heart of a winter Friday night my freshman year, I was dazed and confused when I got a call from my friends to meet them at Est Est Est. Dazedly and confusedly, I began trudging to SSS,* probably the point on campus farthest away. Remarkably, it wasn't until I arrived at the door that I questioned how and why exactly my friends were partying in Yale's administrative building. Of course, they weren't. But it was cold and my ID somehow worked so I went inside SSS to pull out my phone. It was quiet, the old wood creaking and the snow barely visible outside the stained glass. And I sat down. And I looked up. At this giant room I was in. At this place where thousands of people had sat before me. And alone, at night, in the middle of a New Haven storm, I felt so remarkably, unbelievably safe.

---

* Sheffield-Sterling-Strathcona Hall is a Yale building that houses deans' offices and a large lecture hall.

We don't have a word for the opposite of loneliness, but if we did, I'd say that's how I feel at Yale. How I feel right now. Here. With all of you. In love, impressed, humbled, scared. And we don't have to lose that.

We're in this together, 2012. Let's make something happen to this world.

FICTION

The middle of the universe is tonight, is here,
And everything behind is a sunk cost.

—*Marina Keegan, from the poem "Bygones"*

Cold Pastoral

We were in the stage where we couldn't make serious eye contact for fear of implying we were too invested. We used euphemisms like "I miss you" and "I like you" and smiled every time our noses got too close. I was staying over at his place two or three nights a week and met his parents at an awkward brunch in Burlington. A lot of time was spent being consciously romantic: making sushi, walking places, waiting too long before responding to texts. I fluctuated between adding songs to his playlist and wondering if I should stop hooking up with people I was 80 percent into and finally spend some time alone. (Read the books I was embarrassed I hadn't read.) (Call my mother.) The thing is, I like being liked, and a lot of my friends had graduated and moved to cities. I'd thought about ending things but my roommate Charlotte advised me against it. Brian was handsome and smoked the same amount as me, and sometimes in the mornings, I'd wake up and smile first thing because he made me feel safe.

In March, he died. I was microwaving instant Thai soup when I got a call from his best friend asking if I knew which hospital he was at.

"Who?" I said.

"Brian," he said. "You haven't heard?"

* * *

I was in a seminar my senior year where we read poems by John Keats. He has this famous one called "Ode on a Grecian Urn" where these two lovers are almost kissing, frozen with their faces cocked beneath a tree. The tragedy, the professor said, is in eternal stasis. She never fades, they never kiss; but I remember finding the whole thing vaguely romantic. My ideal, after all, was always before we walked home—and ironically, I had that now.

* * *

I watched as the microwave droned in lopsided circles, but I never took the soup out. Someone else must have. Charlotte, perhaps, or one of my friends who came over in groups, offering food in imitation of an adult response and trying to decipher my commitment. I was trying too. I'd made out with a guy named Otto when I was back in Austin over Christmas, and Brian and I had never quite stopped playing games. We were involved, of course, but not associated.

"What's the deal?" people would shout over the music when he'd gone to get a drink and I'd explain that there was no deal to explain.

"We're hanging out," I'd say, smiling. "We like hanging out."

I think we took a certain pride in our ambiguity. As if the tribulations of it all were somehow beneath us. Secretly, of course, the pauses in our correspondence were as calculated as our casualness—and we'd wait for those drunken moments when we might admit a "Hey," pause, "I like you."

"Are you okay?" they asked now. Whispering, almost, as if I were fragile. We sat around that first night sipping singular drinks, a friend turning on a song and then stopping it. I wish I could say I was shocked into a state of inarticulate confusion, but I found myself remarkably capable of answering questions.

"They weren't dating," Sarah whispered to Sam, and I gave a soft smile so they knew it was okay that I'd heard.

But it became clear very quickly that I'd underestimated how much I liked him. Not him, perhaps, but the fact that I had someone on the other end of an invisible line. Someone to update and get updates from, to inform of a comic discovery, to imagine while dancing in a lonely basement, and to return to, finally, when the music stopped. Brian's death was the clearest and most horrifying example of my terrific obsession with the unattainable. Alive, his biggest flaw was most likely that he liked me. Dead, his perfections were clearer.

But I'm not being fair. The fact of the matter is I felt a strange but recognizable hole that grew just behind my lungs. There was a person whose eyes and neck and penis I had kissed the night before and this person no longer existed. The second cliché was that I couldn't quite encompass it. Regardless, I surprised myself that night by crying alone once my friends had left, my face pressed hard against my pillow.

* * *

The first time I saw Lauren Cleaver, she was playing ukulele and singing in a basement lit by strings of plastic red peppers. I remember making two observations during the twenty minutes my friends and I hung around the concert and sipped beers: one, that I wanted her outfit (floral overall shorts and a canvas jacket), and two, that she was skinnier than me, a quality that made her instantly less likable. She was pretty, apart from a very large nose, and I'd seen her around campus, riding her bike along Pear Street or smoking cigarettes out-side the library. She had the rare combination of being quiet and popular, a code that made her intimidating to younger, fashionable girls and mysterious to older, confident boys. We moved in different circles and I hardly thought about her again until the morning after I first kissed Brian, whom she had dated intensely and inseparably for two years and nine months.

I'd never had to deal with an ex-girlfriend before and I didn't like it. Adam and I were each other's firsts and I'd only had month-long things since the two of us broke up. One thing I am is self-aware (to a neurotic fault), and I recognize that a massive percentage of my self-esteem depends on the attention of a series of smug boys at the University of Ver-mont. The problem is I'm good at attracting them: verbally witty and successful at sending texts. I'm also well dressed, or try to be, and make fun of boys in the way that reads as *I like you*. Perhaps it's not a problem so much as a crutch, but I have this pathetic fantasy that I'd be more productive if I were less attractive. Finally finish some paintings or apply for funding of some kind. The point is that Lauren Cleaver and I were not friends because Lauren Cleaver and I had all this in common. This, and Brian.

* * *

His parents arrived the morning after the accident, and his roommates e-mailed a few people they thought might want to stop by. I wanted to go, and felt like I had to go, so I put on a pair of black jeans and a black sweater and asked Charlotte if I could borrow her black boots.

"They don't fit you," she said. "And besides, you don't need to have black shoes."

I wasn't sure. And felt guilty for pondering my red ballet flats as I walked the seven-minute walk to his house. I figured I wasn't supposed to be capable of that kind of thinking, and I felt like an alien. I feel that a lot, actually, in a lot of circumstances. Like I ought to be feeling something I don't. My father used to tease me at the table by implying "cold Claire" had brought in the draft. I had three older sisters, all beautiful, and I was always less affected than they were, slower to smile. I remember finding it extremely hard to open presents as a child because the requisite theatricality was too exhausting. My sisters forever humiliated me over a moment in fifth grade when I'd opened a present from my grandmother and declared, straight-faced, "I already have this."

It was cold for March, so I walked quickly. Brown snow still hugged the sides of our streets and the pines leaned in like gray walls, still limp with yellow Christmas lights. Whenever I slept at Brian's, I called him as soon as I passed this certain stop sign—timing his arrival at the door so I wouldn't have to wait. "I'm here," I'd say, a block away, and he'd meander downstairs to let me in. This time, I knocked.

William let me in. Roommate and rich boy from Los Angeles. We were never friends, really, just occasional cohabiters, but we awkwardly hugged and he asked me how I was.

"Fine," I said instinctively. But he understood that I wasn't.

We walked upstairs and I felt immediately like I shouldn't have been there. It was smaller than I'd imagined: Brian's parents, two adults I didn't recognize, and five or six of his closest friends. They huddled together in the corner next to a plate of bagels and an untouched platter of fruit. His mother was actually sobbing into the side of one of the women and I felt suddenly and extremely claustrophobic. The whole world was stark and bleak and I realized I couldn't think of a single thing I was looking forward to. Brian had begun to be that for me—the thing at the end of the day I could think about when everything else was boring. I looked through the open door to his room and saw that his bed was still unmade.

"This is Claire," William said. Tactful enough to stop before attempting to label my relationship. I held up a palm to the room and I wondered if anyone else had needed to be introduced.

"Claire," his father said. "It's good to see you." He sounded genuine.

We'd gotten along at that brunch, though the whole thing was kind of an accident. Brian and I had slept late and when his parents arrived at his house at eleven o'clock, I was still in his bed, naked. I got dressed quickly—embarrassed to put on my heels from the night before—and was invited by default to eat eggs at Mirabelles. We laughed about it later.

"Good thing you weren't some one-night stand." He bit at my ear.

"Good thing," I said, and punched him.

* * *

Brian's dad gestured toward the untouched food but I said I was fine and moved over to the circle of his friends. I could tell at least one of them, Susannah, didn't want me there. You don't know him, I'm sure she was thinking. We don't know you.

Apparently, they'd all been together at the hospital on Tuesday night and they were sharing stories in hushed voices about how and when they found out and waited, how and when the congenital aneurysm took place. I wanted to ask exactly how it all worked, how it all happened, but I couldn't really engage. I kept looking into Brian's room at the lump of a comforter piled on his sheetless bed, at the light spilling in from his window, speckling its folds, and decided it was the saddest thing I'd ever seen.

* * *

When Lauren Cleaver walked down from upstairs, everyone turned. Her face was swollen and red and she was breathing in staccato bursts. She must have gone upstairs to collect herself. To calm down, stop crying. There was an older boy with her whom I recognized from pictures as Brian's brother. He was holding her by the shoulders and saying something into her ear. My mind raced, imagining the dinners she must have had at his family's table. The trips she might have taken with them, the grandparents she must have met. She'd have watched movies at his real house clad in sweatpants and sweaters. Spent time with his brother, his mother, met his dog, his uncles, his high school friends.

Lauren looked thin and beautiful as she walked down the stairs and I realized that of course I wasn't the girlfriend. I can't explain how or why, but it filled me with a profound, seething anger . . . followed, inevitably, by waves of a familiar self-disgust. Brian was mine, I wanted to cry. My nose he'd kissed on Friday, my shirt he'd slipped his hand inside. The last time he'd kissed Lauren was in June and I knew they no longer talked. I imagined for a moment what he would have been like if Lauren died—if he would have romanticized their relationship and lamented the loss of their potential reunion. But it didn't really seem like she was engaged in rationalization, just that she loved him a lot. Or had.

I knew, of course, that their breakup had been mutual and long coming. Brian and Lauren were beyond associated, and their collapse was slow and necessary. I also knew that only days before, I'd engaged in late-night deliberations with Charlotte over whether or not to break things off—that only days before I didn't think of Brian the way I thought of him now—but neither of those things seemed to matter. Lauren was harrowed, drastically, and my cheeks were smooth and dry. I felt inadequate, cold; my relationship with Brian abruptly grounded.

For some reason I hadn't until just then tried to think of the last time I'd seen him. But it must have been Tuesday morning when I darted out of his room and off to class. I'd forgotten my computer charger so I had to ring the doorbell again and I crawled back into bed fully clothed for a minute before I left. I wished I could remember the last thing he said to me but I couldn't.

* * *

The gathering came to a close around noon when UVM's president (whom none of us had ever seen before) stopped by to give his condolences and explain the logistics of a campus vigil scheduled for a few days later. No one wanted to be the first to leave, but eventually Susannah said she had a rehearsal and kissed Brian's parents on the cheek before heading back into the snow. Others followed suit, and I was pulling on my peacoat when his mother came over and placed a hand on my shoulder.

"Claire," she said, her eyes still welling. "Thank you." I nodded, opening my mouth and then shutting it. "Brian told me about you, you know that? When I'd call him to check in, he'd tell me about you."

I didn't know what to say.

"He was an amazing guy." It sounded so stupid. I wasn't expecting it but something about speaking to her made my face squint up and I covered it with my hands because I'd started to cry. She moved her hand back to my shoulder and I thought about what Brian would think if he could see us.

"James and I were hoping you could say something at the vigil," she said. "William and Adam will be speaking as well and it'd be nice to have you."

"Sure," I nodded again, instinctively.

"Good," she said. "I think he'd like that." There was silence for a minute as she studied me. And it struck me for the first time that she thought I was his girlfriend.

"Sure," I said again, for no reason. Comprehending, finally, what I'd just said I'd do. What I'd just agreed to without thinking.

*   *   *

That night it sleeted. Thick waves of ice rain pelted down on our pines and the Burlington streets were once again reduced to dark slush. Charlotte and our gay friend Kyle sat around my apartment and tried to watch *The Royal Tenenbaums* but abandoned it halfway because the whole thing felt stupid and we felt bad for laughing. Personally, I was trying not to think about the fact that I had to stand up in front of the university in two days and say something about Brian. Stand stupidly with a piece of printed paper as Lauren and the rest of them silently sobbed. I'd probably try to get choked up and fail under pressure.

"Who's she?" a girl would ask.

"Apparently they were hooking up?" her friend would answer. They'd look at each other, wax dripping off their candles and onto their paper cup holders, eyebrows raised.

I had a headache and around three we finally divided off to our beds.

That's when I got it. No subject line; just the name, Lauren Cleaver, bolded in my inbox:

> Hey I have a strange favor to ask that's kind of time sensitive. I'd appreciate if you gave me a call but understand if you don't want to. Let me know if you don't so I can figure out some other way to do this. 9175555837.
>
> L

I called her immediately. It was three A.M. but the message was sent at 2:15 and I didn't feel like waiting. It started ringing and I sat up.

"Hello?" Her voice was strained but clear, and I remembered that she was a singer.

"Hey. It's Claire."

"Hi."

"Hi." There was silence for about five seconds and I wondered if she was trying not to cry. "Do you know where Brian's journal is?"

I didn't know he'd had one but didn't want to admit it. Once again I got strangely possessive, like I had something to prove.

"No," I said. "I don't think so."

"Okay. Well, it should be in the third drawer of his dresser. He should still keep it there."

"All right." I wasn't sure where this was going. I heard the small pop of an inhale and realized she was smoking a cigarette. It made me angry.

"Do you think you could take it?"

"Why?"

"Because he wouldn't want his parents to read it." I paused

and we let silence hang between us again. "I've thought a lot about this. It meant a lot to him. His parents will clean out his room and they'll read it and it will upset them and . . . him."

"Why don't you take it?"

"Because . . . I don't have any reason to go over there." I thought about this for a moment.

"Ask William to take it."

"I don't want William to read it."

"But you want me to?" I was genuinely confused. She paused and I heard her inhale again.

"You're not going to," she said. It was a command, not a question, and I didn't like the way she was talking to me. I'd always thought she was shyer, soft. "Call William and tell him you left some clothes there you want to pick up . . . you did sleep there, right?"

I didn't say anything. Neither did she. I kept the phone pressed to my ear but it sounded like she'd moved it away from her face and I wondered again if she was trying not to cry.

"Listen," she said finally. "Just. He wouldn't want his parents to read it, okay? They wouldn't want to read it. There's shit in there about them and him and—if you can't do it I'll just figure something else out." I imagined for a second the way I'd first seen her: singing in that basement with the ukulele and red-pepper lights. She'd seemed so cool, so non-chalant. I wondered if she'd hooked up with someone after that show. Not Brian, obviously, but some other boy with an unshaven face. I wondered if he was in her life now. If she had some guy whose bed she looked forward to when everything was boring. If he knew where she'd been that morning and how he'd felt about it.

"Fine," I said. "I'll do it."

"Thank you." There was silence again and I wasn't sure if I

was supposed to hang up. I wondered if she knew I was speaking at the vigil, but figured she must have. I thought about saying something but didn't, and we stayed on the line for a while longer, cross-legged on our beds.

"Bye," she said suddenly, and hung up before I could respond. I meant to go to bed but I couldn't sleep—and found myself clicking through all seven hundred of her Facebook photos before I passed out with my hand on my laptop.

* * *

The question of whether or not I was going to read it wasn't a question. As soon as I had the worn leather journal—slipped out, as predicted, from his third dresser drawer—I went into our central library and up into the stacks. I'd taken a sweater as well, a plain green one he wore a lot but that wasn't distinct enough to be recognized as his, and put it on, which made me feel both sad and safe. I sat at an old desk and opened it from the back, flipping until I saw my name for the first time. His sentences were short, unembellished, repetitive, and it was clear he wasn't lying to anybody. I scanned quickly, eyes sliding back and forth across the pages, reading paragraphs, excerpts, lists:

> I'm acting weird. I know I'm choosing to distract myself. The Claire thing feels uncertain. A distraction. Re: Lauren, I feel like I'm still not comprehending it all. I act like everything is fine and even now I choose to deal with Claire stuff instead of . . .
>
> Lauren on Saturday: I sent her a g-chat to which she didn't respond (she was at band rehearsal), then texted her. She responded upon leaving, then I responded, then she either didn't respond or did while my phone was

dead. Then I e-mailed her and she may or may not have seen it but didn't respond and . . .

Lately I've felt a kind of numbness. Like this feeling like I'm faking it all—but maybe it's just because I'm used to being in love. Like I can hug her and move my fingers along her neck but it's not real. There's no emotional desire for closeness. She feels it too I think but it's funny because I wait for her text messages, hoping she'll contact me and get really pissed and insecure when she doesn't. I know she waits before responding which is . . .

I need to slow things down. I won't hook up with other people if I have her as an option and I shouldn't be entering something serious again. But then again, it's like what William said with his whole "why change options if this one is good" approach. I like Claire. Maybe I need to stop lying to myself about that. I want a girl that's full of life and enthusiasm and optimism and creativity and assumed profundity. Who I do not have to brag to. Who I can engage in a dialogue. I want honesty, more than anything, probably because Lauren and I lost that. I just don't think Claire is that person—too sort of sad all the time and self-deprecating. Or maybe she is, and I just need time to myself to . . .

I worried a lot this week that Lauren might actually be the right girl for me long term, which was depressing because I haven't had to deal with that whole mindset for a while . . . Not that I made a mistake in breaking up with her. But in that we might have ruined the potential for a future together of some kind. It needed to end for now. THE relationship needed to end for this time of our lives. But it's obvious I'm not over HER as a person, I just need to admit it. (I know she feels the same.) She had a gig in Laurence the other day and I nearly felt sick thinking about the guys who'd be there to . . .

I had a dream last night where Claire and I were in a Lauren/Brian state of our relationship. She didn't want to hang out with me (or I sensed that) and I was compensating by being pathetic and always acting, like pretending that I was happy and cool and fun because I felt insecure about how she felt about me. I'm starting to think Claire should just be my girlfriend!? I don't know what it is. Maybe I'm just exhausted. BUT it also diminishes the fantasy. Why CAN'T we? Maybe it implies there's something wrong with the relationship. Some reason . . .

I almost feel like I'm settling. I dunno. Maybe I'm just not totally over Lauren (true), maybe I'm just unsure about her on a more fundamental level. The fear of course is to start dating Claire and then not stop. I just need to find out if she can be imaginative and interesting and spontaneous and make me laugh and want to build something together. BE something. I guess I'm not crazy about her. Or don't really know how I feel. She's sort of into pretension and that's unattractive. She just has this look on her face a lot. Sort of aloof and wide eyed and her lips purse slightly when she's looking somewhere or reading the computer. And it just really turns me off. I look at her at those times and I just think like, fuck, I need to get out of this. And then I feel bad about it because part of me really does like her. Lauren was hotter—or at least had a better body (more in shape). And the sex was better. But it's probably because Claire's so clearly insecure when she's naked and . . .

I went into the bathroom and threw up. I rinsed my mouth in the sink but felt nauseous again and returned to the toilet to vomit a second time, and sat down on the toilet, pressing my fingers into my forehead. I'd never felt so disgusting in my life. Not disgusting—but vacant, punched, like someone had taken a wrench and shoved it into my stomach and twisted it around. I tried to remember that I'd had thoughts like that too. Tried to recount the pros-and-cons list Charlotte and I'd discussed from the depths of my bedroom: he was over-emotional, too cocky, didn't shower enough. And I'd had better sex too. But it didn't matter.

I walked out of the bathroom and down the narrow stair-cases through the books and emerged onto the street and the blaring sun. I opened my phone to call Charlotte but realized I wouldn't know what to say. I walked a few blocks down Pear Street, passing people who didn't know me, and felt anonymous and fat. I stopped when I got to the quad and turned around because I had no destination in mind; I thought about texting Kyle but realized, again, that the prospect of articulation was too exhausting. I think the one thing I really wanted in that moment was to text Brian and crawl into his bed; complain about Brian and the vigil and his death and fall asleep with his arms pulled around me and my hair tangling against his sheets. I took out my phone and called Lauren Cleaver.

"Hello?" she said.

And I hung up.

* * *

That night, I got really fucked up. I had four drinks before we got to the party and did a couple of lines in the bathroom, which I hardly ever do. Spencer was the one with the coke, always was, and he dragged me and Kyle in behind him and locked the door.

"Claire bear," he said. "Claire darling, you're first, you poor thing." He was gayer than Kyle and the two of us exchanged a look.

"We're not talking about it," Kyle said. "That's the rule."

"That's not the rule," I snapped. "You're making me sound like such an asshole."

This time Kyle and Spencer exchanged the looks and I remembered then that they'd hooked up a few times sophomore year. I'd expected everyone at the party to be sympathizing, offering condolences, but it turned out to be the opposite. I think they were all afraid to approach me or figured it wasn't their place. That, or fewer people knew about Brian and me than I'd thought.

"Hey, I'm gonna go," I said, attempting to be genuine. "I'm fine, really, I'll see you guys in a minute."

"Clairee," Spencer cooed.

"Look, I'm fine," I said again. "I'm actually feeling great."

And I was. The coke had me instantly angry and empowered. Fuck Brian, I thought now. Fuck Brian and Lauren and his parents and his vigil. It was unfair of them to involve me in all of this and I wanted to scream at one of them, steal a car and drive home to Austin. I would never tell Lauren what Brian had written about her. Never tell her that all this time he was still thinking about her. Doubting their decision, hoping she might text him. I imagined she must have been doing the same thing—loving him alone at night, thinking of him while she was with other guys—and denying her that knowledge, denying her something, gave me pleasure.

The music pulsed and I wove through bodies and red cups

looking for faces I knew. I felt confident now, defiant, and I wanted a circle of people to enter. To tell a story to and hear them laugh. But I couldn't seem to find anyone I really recognized, and the faces crammed in the living room of 398 Brown Street seemed younger than ever.

"Who are these people?!" I shouted to a boy next to me. I'd never seen him before in my life.

"What!?" he shouted back.

"I said, who are these people? I feel like they're all eighteen!"

"What!?" he said again. But this time he walked past me, shrugging, and I went back into the bathroom where Kyle and Spencer were making out.

"Oh, sorry," I said, backing away, but Kyle opened the door again a second later.

"Come on," he said, taking my shoulders. "Let's go home."

* * *

I woke up the next morning with a headache behind my left eye and thought seriously about calling Brian's mother and telling her I just couldn't do it. That it was going to be too hard. But I think part of me, deep down, wanted to do it, because I didn't call all morning and by the time the sun set again, I knew it was too late to cancel. I had to prepare something and that was that.

I opened a Word document and stared at it for a few hours. Charlotte kept bringing me food because she wanted to help and didn't know what else to do—but I let most of it sit cold by my computer, Brian's musings on my body still fresh in my mind. We watched the end of *The Royal Tenenbaums* around four (Charlotte thought I could use a fresh start), but I was as lost afterward as I had been before. I played with the idea of framing the whole thing in Keats's Grecian Urn—talking about how there was something romantic in preservation at a moment of static bliss. But the whole thing felt like an English paper and I realized a note of optimism might actually be inappropriate.

Around ten P.M. I started to panic. The pressure of the deadline, of the task I had to complete, clarified my already numb condition. I was upset and anxious and overwhelmed—no longer by the circumstances themselves, but by my mandate to assess them. How was I feeling? How were we all supposed to be feeling? What did Brian's death say about our generation? The ephemeral nature of life? The need to cherish?

I gave up on profundity and tried writing honestly. Brian was an amazing guy. Even when he was busy with his own work and issues, he always took the time to listen. But every time I wrote these sentences, phrases from his notebook echoed back at me. "I almost feel like I'm settling." "There's no emotional desire for closeness." "Lauren was hotter—Claire's so clearly insecure when she's naked." They pierced me, deeply, and I entered a realm of insecurity I'd never been in before, wary of acknowledging it. I hated Lauren Cleaver more than I'd hated anyone in my entire life and I thought a lot that day about whether she'd sent me to pick up his journal on purpose. Knowing I'd read it, knowing I'd get hurt. But I remembered how swollen her face was, how raw her eyes had been, and had another thought entirely: that she'd asked me in an act of self-protection. Scared of what she might read. Scared of the rejection she might discover.

* * *

I was about to give in for the night and resolve to wake up early when I got another subjectless e-mail in my inbox:

Hey.

Thanks for today. I know Brian would be very grateful.

I'm sorry if I was cold last night—it's been an extremely hard few days for me, obviously. But I ought to acknowledge this is also hard for you.

I've attached a document with some thoughts you might be able to use tomorrow. No pressure if you're all set, but I figured I owe you one.

L

I opened the attachment. There were lyrics from his favorite songs, a copy of a poem he wrote freshman year. Things he'd said about what he wanted to be when he "grew up," a link to a funny op-ed he wrote in the school newspaper. There were also bullets she'd written up describing him— endearingly confident, full of a genuine wonder, contagiously enthused.

I didn't want to be, but I was grateful. I kept it open beside my other document and began writing. I clicked on the link to his article, listened to the songs she mentioned, and jotted down lyrics. I was so relieved and distracted by the new material that it wasn't until thirty minutes later that I thought about Lauren for the first time without also thinking about myself. She loved Brian. It was so remarkably, indubitably clear. And whether or not he understood it, he'd loved her back. At first I'd thought it was a favor, some kind of thank-you for picking up the journal. But as I scrolled through her document again I realized it had nothing to do with helping me. Nothing.

* * *

I finished a draft of my remarks and took a shower for the first time in two days. My hair was tangled and matted in the back, and it took me nearly twenty minutes to pick it apart with my pruned fingers. Halfway through, I became exhausted and sat cross-legged on the floor of the shower, the water pelting down on my hunched back, echoing up and filling my head with nothing but its steady pounding. When I got out, I put on Brian's sweater and got back into bed. I was going to tell her. Let her know what Brian had written—let her read it for herself. Just so you know, I would write in an e-mail, he still loved you all along.

But before I opened my computer I leaned over and pulled Brian's journal out of my backpack. It was long, enviably full, and this time I opened to a part near the beginning. I was tired and hurt and the headache behind my left eye had never quite vanished—but I read the love story of Lauren Cleaver and Brian Jones until 5:30 that morning.

* * *

The service was uneventful. Five or six hundred students gathered on the main green at 7:30 the next night and the chaplain's office handed out small candles tucked inside paper cups. I wondered if they recycled these from vigil to vigil but abandoned the thought when I was led to stand with William, Adam, and Brian's parents. They said their pieces and I said mine, his mother struggling to contain herself when she briefly addressed the students and thanked the school. When I took the podium, I was worried people would whisper or wonder why I was speaking, but they didn't. I'm not even sure they distinguished what I said from the others. I'd spent the first half of the vigil searching the crowd for Lauren's face but I couldn't find her and wondered if she'd decided not to show up. But just before I began speaking, I saw her strawberry blonde hair somewhere near the back left—illuminated and glowing from the light of her small candle. When I quoted his article, the audience emitted a small laugh, and when I read from his favorite song, they got quiet. Endearingly confident, I said, full of a genuine wonder, contagiously enthused. I looked right at her when I said that, and she nodded.

When it ended, they had these bagpipes play, and I waited around with the others as the students slowly blew out their candles, walking over waxed grass to their dorm rooms and libraries. Lauren came to say good-bye to his family but I could see now that she felt as uncomfortable with her role around them as I did.

I chased her down before she had a chance to leave the gate.

"Hey," I said.

"Hi." We stood there for a second, silent.

"Thank you. That was . . . he would have liked it."

"Thank *you*," I said awkwardly. "For the stuff."

"No problem." She looked down. "I wasn't sure you were going to use any of it. You didn't get back to me." I didn't say anything. I looked at her and realized that she'd started crying again, silently.

I thought about the things he'd said about her in his journal. The morning after they first kissed when he'd spent forty minutes writing her a three-line e-mail. The game of bowling where they got high in the bathroom, the way he'd described her collarbone and her smile and the first time he saw her band play in the basement during the storm. The first time they had sex and didn't use a condom and the first time he came home with her for Thanksgiving and met her alcoholic mother and the discussion they'd had about it afterward. How he'd said he held her and told her it'd be okay and that he'd always be there. The bad poem he wrote for her and the good song she wrote for him. The time they thought she was pregnant and the time his grandfather died. How they'd said how much they loved each other and how they always would. How he worried he loved her more than she loved him and that she had a crush on a boy named Emmanuel. And I thought then of how he'd described things growing old. Growing similar, habitual. How he'd begun to wake up in the morning without rolling over to kiss her. How he'd started to resent the time away from his friends, her nagging habits. How he'd begun to look at other girls and compare her to the hypothetical. How she'd begun to ignore him too and how they'd gone along anyway for another six months, another year. How it'd ended and how he'd felt free and young and energized. But then how he'd begun to miss her. And doubt himself. And worry that they'd screwed things up forever. How he'd loved her, still, whether or not he understood it, and how, when it came down to it, I could never really compare.

I had their story in my bag. The secret that he, too, had never let things go. Had it tucked inside his journal with a note I'd slipped inside. Thanking her. Telling her I didn't want to talk to her again because it would be too hard. But I looked at her then, with the tears dripping slowly down her thin cheeks, and I knew, in the end, it'd be better if I kept it. Better if she never knew.

"I'm sorry," I said. It was all I could get out. "I'm so sorry," I said. And walked away.

* * *

That night I went out again. Charlotte, Kyle, and I went to a party down on Pear and I saw this guy named Marshall, who I knew from my Russian lit class, when we were both on the fire escape, getting some air. I usually don't smoke but I bummed a cigarette off him and when he gave it to me he half smiled. Marshall was handsome. Smart. And suddenly, more than anything I'd ever wanted in my life, I wanted him to love me. I stayed out there with him for nearly an hour and we talked about a lot of things and moved closer and closer together. Eventually, we were both shivering and he asked if I wanted to go back to his apartment with him. I did. I'd never wanted anything more. But as I watched him smile back at me and zip his coat, I saw everything in the world build up and then everything in the world fall down again.

Winter Break

I was stoned when I saw the eskimoed figure crunching down the street with a flashlight and a cocker spaniel. The iced trees hung in on the road and my dazed synapses made suburbia look like a cave. The figure trudged ahead as I flexed my stiff fingers, watching mutely from my hot box of dry heat and public radio. I'd forgotten Michigan's stillness while I was at school—the way houses slept and trucks made patterns in the snow. So I turned off the speakers and let my car slow to a stop. All that moved was the yellow beam of my mother's flashlight, flicking up and down as she walked, jerking my dog away from pinecones and driveways and someone else's pee.

I told my parents I'd be getting in at ten so I'd have time to visit Sam before they knew I was home. When I got to his house we went straight to his room and got in bed with our clothes on, pressing our faces together without even kissing. "I'm here," I said, and we curled in disbelief. It was our first long-distance reunion and I finally understood the addiction of self-deprivation.

We stayed there for an hour before I dragged myself out of bed and back into my car, lingering with him in the passenger seat as the windows frosted and we passed a thin joint. "Don't leave," he said, biting at my shoulder. "You're always leaving." I exhaled slowly and leaned my head against his neck. The thought of sleeping in his bed tore at the image of my mother waiting in the kitchen with baked goods that were already cold.

"Tomorrow," I said, squeezing his hand and sitting up. "I have to spend my first night at home."

For a while, she didn't see me. I'm not sure why I waited in my car but for some reason I didn't feel like moving. Winters turned our town into a black-and-white wonderland and I liked watching my mom pad through its tunneled core. She was overdressed, peering out from an astronautic parka, two scarves, and a pair of thick leather mittens. Yet she managed a kind of mid-road grace, unconcerned that a car could disturb her migration. She did it three times a day. Strapped up my spaniel and circled the block. When my brothers and I begged for the dog, we'd sworn to switch off in rotating shifts. But by the time it was big we were busy with homework or friends or that project we had to start now.

I rolled down my window and felt a flood of cold air on my face. My dog let out a small howl, twigs cracked in the woods, and something about the stillness or my state of mind reminded me of the world's remarkable capacity to carry on in every place at once. I thought of my mother circling suburbia while I drank in dim fraternities or video-chatted with Sam or slept lazily in my dorm while it snowed out my window. I loved her at that moment in a way that twisted my stomach.

"Mom!" I shouted from the side of my car. The dog barked and she snapped around, frozen like a deer in my car's white light. She stared for a second, struggling to see through the blinding headlights. I saw something then that I hadn't seen before, or if I had, I'd chosen to ignore. There was a frailty to her posture, a thinness in her cheeks. She looked tired and cold for the instant before she lit up in motion, jogging slightly toward the hum of my car. But I didn't think about it because I was happy and I loved her and for the most part, I don't like the kind of revelations I have when I'm high.

When I woke up the next morning, my mom was in the basement sorting socks. I was glad to be home and it was nice to be reminded of the places our floors creaked. My semester at school had been decent but I'd missed home in a new way I could only attribute to Sam. We'd met that summer while working at the lake, and I'd romanticized Michigan so much that it hung on our phone calls. My dad liked to say we were in the center of the center, but upstate Erie wasn't exactly downtown. In August, Sam and I took the eighteen-hour train to New York, curling on window seats and sharing an iPod. After that I craved the camaraderie of cities. Energy and art and all-nighters. When I told my dad he said New York was cheap and my parents laughed about never going back.

But this was the time when I found everything romantic. I granted the world a kind of strange generosity. Ideas convinced me and ordinary activities had an almost giddy newness. Part of it was probably the pot. Smoking before anything gave an excuse for a good time. We could go skating or bowling without feeling lame. So we passed bowls in the back of my car and alternated between overanalysis and blank stares. In July I'd get home late and my dad would be in the kitchen, drunk and finally eating.

Microwavable sausage links, cold cuts, tubs of ice cream with the ring of measuring spoons. Sometimes I'd warm up some pasta and sit with him as he watched *CSI*. But other times I'd ask him why he was up at three and smell his sodas while his head was in the fridge.

I went down and sat on the rug next to my mom. My trash bags of dirty dorm clothes were already folded in neat piles by the shelf. She looked young for fifty—thin, blonde, and still able to twist her legs behind her while she searched for striped blues, Green Bay greens, and the nuances of whites. We talked for a while about classes and food. At little party things or parent-teacher meetings, people would tell us our expressions were the same. I'd never really noticed it on my own—I just thought the way she smiled made sense.

"So tell me about Sam," she said. I knew we'd land on it eventually. "I hardly got to meet him before you left for school."

"Yeah you did," I said, rebraiding my hair. "We hung out here all the time."

"Maybe."

"Not maybe, yes."

"Okay, yes." She opened the dryer and eased some sheets into a basket. "But you know what I mean. What's he like?"

"Um, he's great," I said. "He studies astronomy at Eastville, but might drop it and just do something with reading."

"Wow."

"Yeah. He's pretty smart. It's nice, we actually talk about real stuff. Not like Chris."

She smiled. "And you stayed together all semester? You didn't even . . ." Her voice trailed off.

"Uh, no," I said affirmatively. I waited for a second to see how she'd react. "I'm actually offended that you said that."

"Addie, I didn't mean to be offensive, I'm just saying that's a long time without seeing each other." I realized then that it was a genuine sentiment. I traced back through the fragments I'd heard of my mother's life before my dad, trying to remember whether long distances had been involved.

"Kind of," I said.

"Did you get together with anyone at school?"

"No. Mom, I don't want to talk about this, it's not like that. And don't say 'get together.'" She looked hurt and I already felt bad.

"Okay. 'Have a crush.' Sorry, I didn't realize how serious it was. That's great, honey."

"Yeah." I waited for a second, wondering if it was fair to continue. "It was really nice to have someone around all the time, you know? Not around around, but like, texting me and thinking about me when I was in class or like, at some party."

"That's romantic." Again there was a genuineness in her eyes that I felt in my stomach.

"Where's Dad?"

"Asleep."

"He's asleep? It's like ten A.M."

She shrugged. "You should try to play with your brother at some point. He's been asking when you'll get home." She liked this. Her children were spaced such that they all got along. My brothers and I never had a chance to beat each other up—we were always too young or too old.

My family was like anyone's, just functional enough to be functional. It wasn't until college that I really realized everyone's house had its own messed-up stories. (Kaylie's brother did coke and Max's dad was secretly gay.) We had nothing like that. Perhaps the problem was we didn't have much at all. My older brothers worked in Chicago, and Kyle was the only kid home. Our parents didn't fight in the conventional way, mostly because I don't think they thought it was worth it. For as long as I can remember, my mom woke up at six to work out and on her ten thousand projects. She ate lettuces and soy things but cooked real food for the rest of us. My dad had a job in car sales and was really skinny. My brothers and I hardly recognized the muscular man standing next to our mom in their wedding photos. I knew it bothered her. The problem was that he meant really well. That's the thing, he just meant really well.

As for me, I didn't know what I wanted. Cigarette holes had started spotting the sides of my skirts and the semester had granted a profundity to the world that I could photograph or turn into a bad poem. Everything seemed worthy of retelling and I'd struggle to stop stories before I started. But my professional ambitions were still switching with the channels of my illegal downloads. Wide-eyed and coiled in bed, Sam and I would be convinced by the dramas of forty-six minutes—idealizing the pursuits of doctors, politicians, astronauts in space. Bored or exhausted with regularity, we'd envy *House* and *Law and Order*, cuddling away our apathy until we were reminded that all we really wanted was to lie in bed. I was in love for the first time and my mother could tell.

I passed my little brother Kyle's room on the way back upstairs. He didn't have any lights on and was buried with headphones in a game of World of Warcraft.

"What's up?" I said, leaning in his doorway. He didn't hear me so I said it again. "What's up, geek?" He turned around in his swivel chair.

"Hey."

"What are you doing tonight?" I asked. He'd gone back to the game, shooting some blue whirlwind of a spell out of his character's hands.

"Nothing."

"But didn't you just get out for winter break?"

"Yeah."

"Cool." I stayed leaning in the doorway, remembering the

basement parties I'd attended in eighth grade. When we'd sip on Evian bottles of vodka and gag through truth or dare.

"Do you want to jump on the trampoline later?" He was still facing the screen, sliding and clicking his left hand as he typed hard with the right. "I got all the snow off on Tuesday." I looked at his mop of brown hair, glowing slightly green from his monitor.

"Ugh, I can't," I said, walking toward his desk. "I promised Sam I'd go over."

"Okay." He took a swig from a root beer by his keyboard.

I couldn't leave. "Wait, so who are you fighting? Is that a troll or something?"

"It's an Ogre. But my usual character is a Blood Elf."

"Nice," I said. "That dude reminds me of *Avatar*."

"Not really," he half scoffed. "Are you going to be here tomorrow?"

"Yeah, yeah," I said. "I'm coming home in the morning."

"Nice." I waited. He killed something that looked like a fanged bull. "So how're Mom and Dad? Bothering you enough?"

"I guess." I was annoying him at this point. "Mom's obsessed with my homework."

I laughed. "What about Dad?"

He waited for a minute until he started clicking again. "Um, the same. He's kind of drinking a lot." I hadn't expected this. But I knew he was smart and it was stupid to think he didn't know what was going on. I waited by his computer for a few seconds until I punched him in the shoulder and walked toward the door.

"Keep the lights on in here," I said, pausing in the doorway to hit the switch. "It's creepy if you hang out in the dark."

"Okay." He stayed looking at the screen as I went into my

room to change into sexier underwear before I left for Sam's. Then I was gone.

That night we went to the lake and walked out to its center, where we passed a spliff and talked about the fate of humanity. Sam had a lot of opinions about the universe shrinking back up and banging again but I didn't really have a view one way or another. I liked listening to him, though. The ice was thick enough to hold the fishermen's trucks but there was still something sexy about lying down where we used to canoe. I went to college in Ohio, but Sam's school was just down the street. The weed urged me to ask him if he ever came here with anyone else, but it started to snow a little so I leaned backward instead. He did too, and our noses touched.

"This is good," he said.

"I know."

"I wish it was just us."

"I know," I said.

We waited there for a while until our heads cleared and our butts froze. He didn't need to explain what he meant because he knew I knew he was talking about everything.

When we got back to his house we took a shower and fell dizzily asleep before our hormones could even take over.

The next day I dragged him with me when I went back to my house. He wanted to stay at his place for the day because he had a bigger TV and his parents weren't home. But I told him that I'd left at lunch and gotten in late and besides, we're always at your house and you know it. When we pulled into my driveway my dad was shoveling the steps, which was surprising. He had on a giant windbreaker and we could see the spots where it darkened under his arms. I felt the familiar twist of sympathetic embarrassment and then embarrassment that I'd felt that in the first place.

My mom came out from the computer room and we all talked in the kitchen for a while. She lingered even after my dad went back out to shovel, rearranging papers and mentioning cool articles she'd read online. She was watching us, and I knew she was soaking in our every expression.

"What do your parents do, Sam?"

"They work at the school."

"Addie tells me you're studying science."

"Yes, ma'am, at least for now." He looked teasingly at me and I reached a hand at his stomach, pulling his shirt so he moved closer and put his arms around my sides. I meant it as a gesture of trust, to show my mother we were comfortable around her. But she looked at us for a second, lost, and then went to check something on her phone.

"I need to make a call anyway, so you two can go upstairs." She was moving now, looking in the pantry and opening some drawers. "But thanks for talking to your old mother." It was an honest joke and she stopped her motion to smile.

"I love you," I cooed, laughing as we moved out of the kitchen.

"You don't."

"I do! I do!"

Winter break passed us with trips up the stairs. We slept in wearing woolen socks and woke up sweaty. Most of the time I slept at Sam's because his feet poked out the end of my twin-size bed. My mom was usually asleep by the time I drove over there, but I could tell it bothered her anyway. I knew because she'd mention breakfast foods I might like around nine. I think my dad found the whole thing vaguely inappropriate; he was uncertain how to respond to his daughter wrapped up in something serious. But he liked Sam okay and whenever he came by I made sure they had at least ten minutes to talk about hockey. One night when Sam was staying over, my dad walked in while we were watching *Planet Earth*. It was episode two and our interests were shifting from vampire squids to my bed, but my dad asked if it was okay if he joined us. He was drinking and had a bowl of sugar-free Jell-O.

"Sure," I said, shifting up so Sam's arm was merely around my shoulder.

"Cool," he said, and sat down on the opposite couch. This kind of thing never happened at Sam's because his parents were usually doing work or downstairs. We started episode three and our thoughts turned back to the weird things that glowed in the bottom of the ocean. But my dad fell asleep after ten minutes, snoring loud enough that I would have laughed if I were still in high school. Sam and I shut off the TV and I placed a blanket on my dad, throwing away his bowl of Jell-O when we walked upstairs. There was an awkwardness to the way he'd asked to join us that I couldn't get out of my head. Some kind of cafeteria-table solitude that made me want to throw up. I thought then about how most things are not really anyone's fault. I almost shared this with Sam but he was already in my room taking off his shoes. It was nearly two but I could see the glow of Kyle's monitor as I passed by his door.

Sometimes we'd take a day off and I'd spend time alone or with my family. My mom and I went shopping a few times at the mall in Hammond Bay and I helped her make a cheesecake with lemon and ginger. On a cold Tuesday, my older brothers lumbered home in a carpool from Chicago and we all went out to buy a Christmas tree. Toby and Zach were older and immune to the islands they'd left floating in our house. So they laughed and teased and Kyle and I lurked behind them, refreshingly reduced to our attempts to impress. The holiday came and went like it seemed to every year since I was thirteen. We slept till a depressing 9:30 on Christmas morning, though I suspect my little brother woke up earlier to look at the stockings before creeping back upstairs until the rest of us woke up. Sam bought me a necklace with a tiny silver acorn that my mother held off my neck more than once that afternoon. I gave her a crème brûlée torch and a fleece jacket that felt both perfect and stupid the moment she gasped with gratitude.

My anxiety came back on the twenty-sixth and I started dreading the idea of phone calls every time I saw Sam. The vacation had seemed an eternity, but something about the other side of Christmas made college slip back into my consciousness. Once, when Sam was at school, he'd texted me that he couldn't talk because his roommates were sleeping. Smiling to myself, I'd called him anyway—speaking one-way for a whole eight minutes. This is what happened today. This is how I'm feeling. This is why I love you.

Toby and Zach went back to the city and my house returned to its hidey-holes. I went to this horrible yoga class a few times with my mom, but we giggled about the instructor's adjectives afterward, which made us feel like sisters. My dad would accidentally fall asleep on the couch a few times a week and I cringed to think what kind of clichés this spawned in Kyle's head. Dad and I would talk sometimes after I'd driven home late in my smoky sedan. There wasn't much to say but we could get at least ten minutes if I asked him to fill me in on the episode that was on. Once when one had ended and we'd finished a bowl of popcorn, he paused for a minute and looked down at our dog.

"So your mother seems to think you and this Sam kid are awfully happy." She must have brought it up.

"Yeah," I said. "We are."

"She said he bought you that necklace." He gestured loosely at my neck.

"Yeah. For Christmas."

He nodded, almost got up, but then stayed in his chair. "I thought that wind chime I got for her was good." He looked up at me expectantly. It's silver, my mom would have said. He bought her something silver.

"No, it was." I cleared my throat. "That was a really cool gift."

"I'm going to hang that up tomorrow."

I nodded this time. "Yeah, you totally should. That thing's supposed to be cool."

"I'll do that tomorrow," he repeated, walking over to the sink.

He didn't. And by the time either of us woke up my mom's banana bread was cold.

Sam's uncle had an annual New Year's party in Canada, and in a gesture of romantic formality Sam suggested we dress up and drive there instead of getting drunk in someone's basement. He showed me pictures from the previous year while we waited for our instant cookies to bake. Everyone was wearing suits and had champagne and he said that people were maybe going to go skiing the next day. I decided to spend some of my campus job money on a dress and went back to a store I'd seen in the Hammond Bay Galleria. I stood alone in a three-way mirror, unable to choose between a green and two blacks. So I angled the panels and took pictures of each on my phone, sending them one by one in texts to my mom. I had to call her twice to explain how to open them, but she'd said the green made my legs look good so I went with that.

On the day Sam and I were supposed to leave, I found her again folding socks downstairs. I came in wearing the green dress to model it in person.

"What do you think?" I said, spinning around.

"You look beautiful," she said. "He won't be able to keep it on you."

"Mom, come on!" I laughed, turning around. "Can you unzip me?"

She unzipped me and I went back upstairs to pack it away, returning in a pair of jeans and a gray sweater.

"So you're driving up tonight?"

"This afternoon, yeah." I reached my hand into the basket and started searching for a sock with two black stripes. "Don't worry, I'm driving."

"Okay."

"Are you doing anything?"

"Probably not." She smiled. "I don't really like New Year's, it's sort of an excuse to drink."

"Fair enough." We didn't say anything for a while, both absorbed in the sock pairings. "You know your father didn't always drink like this, right?" She was looking right at me and I had to make eye contact.

"I know," I said. "He hasn't been that bad while I've been home, actually. I sort of see him sometimes when you're already asleep."

"That's nice of you to say," she said, this time not smiling. "I don't know, Addie." She let out a sigh. "I just don't know." I hated this kind of discussion and I hated myself for hating it. I wondered for a moment who else my mom might confide in but I wasn't actually sure how close she was with any of her book-group friends. "I don't know if I can do this anymore." She was looking down again.

"Yeah."

"Having you home, it made me think, and you seem so . . ."

"I didn't mean . . ." But I trailed off too. I wasn't sure whether this was different.

She paused. "Now that you guys are almost grown up, I'm not sure there's a point."

"I don't know." It was a stupid response and I wasn't sure if I should comfort her.

There wasn't sadness in her voice, just that same exhaustion I'd seen from my car. My phone vibrated and I flipped it open to a message from Sam.

"You can take that if you want," my mom said, looking down.

"Oh, no, it's fine, it's not a call."

"A text message?" She took pride in knowing the term.

"Yeah."

She paused. "What's it say?" I pressed Open and waited for a second. It was a heart, followed by a message that said "thinking of you." I couldn't show her.

"It's from Sarah," I said. "She wants to know what I'm doing tonight." She looked at me again.

"It's not from Sarah, Addie. It's from Sam."

"No, it's from Sarah, I swear. It says: 'Hey what are you up to later?'"

She smiled for a second but it didn't reach her eyes. "When are you leaving?" Her tone was different. It was cheery, bright. I looked at my watch. It was 1:40 and Sam was picking me up at two.

"You know, Mom, I don't have to—" But she cut me off. "Addie, come on." She pulled her hair back into a bun. "Three more pairs and I'll let you free." So I made three more pairs.

Sam and I smoked two joints on the drive, listening to airy

playlists titled with combinations of our names. Three miles from Canada, we parked the car in a field and let the smoky air out just to be safe, sitting on the hood and holding hands. The air was crisp and the sky seemed determined to be bluest on this last day of the year. We could see mountains from where we were sitting and climbed back into our seats only when the sun started tilting west.

I made Sam leave our room while I put on the green dress so it would be a surprise when I came out. It did make my legs look good and I had to take it off and put it back on again before dinner. Sam smiled at me while we met aunts and old high school friends, our glances exchanging thousands of inside jokes. The night was a whirl of champagne and stupid hats and explaining why and where I went to school. At midnight, everyone gathered in a room with a fire, counting down in an iconic chant. Sam had one arm on the small of my back and I could smell the alcohol and perfume and fire that filled the room. I looked down at the fingers squeezing mine and something about the noise or his smile filled me with a kind of sick understanding of what our hand-holding had done. Of what she was trying to tell me before I got into his car. I tried to focus on the lights of the dying Christmas tree and the shrieking faces of guests I didn't know. But in those final seconds my mind wandered to my dad, who was probably sitting alone in the kitchen, drunk and watching the ball drop on TV; my brother, shooting spells from the depths of his bedroom, his small face green with the glow of his computer; and my mother, crunching down the street with a flashlight and my cocker spaniel, moving through the snowy darkness as the clock hit zero.

Reading Aloud

On Mondays and Wednesdays at 4:30 P.M., Anna takes off her clothes and reads to Sam. Reads him cable-box directions and instant-soup instructions, unpaid bills and pages from his textbooks. Each week she peels off her garments one by one, arranging them beside her chair with practiced stealth. Usually, Sam makes an exotic tea and they revel in descriptions from their mutual senses; it smells like cinnamon berries, it tastes like honey smoke, it feels warmer today. Both can hear its soft percolation, but only Anna can see its cloudy mauve whirlpool. Only Anna can see her wilting breasts and her varicose veins. So she looks at him and he looks at nothing. And they let the words lift off the pages of the manuals and brochures and cereal-box backs and float fully formed from the sixty-something naked woman to the twenty-something blind man.

* * *

Her doctor suggested it. The reading, not her wardrobe choice. Said something about the benefits of purpose or the advantages of routine. Anna was sick and she knew it. Ever since her husband un-retired, she'd had an ache in her left knee joint and she sometimes felt nauseous. For four days last April, she was convinced unquestionably of her pulmonary tuberculosis; for three days in June of her endometrial cancer. She'd taken to leaving an old copy of *The Diagnostic Almanac* on her bedside table, flipping ardently through its pages. Naturally, she'd verify each hypothesis with recurrent appointments. Anna liked her doctor and his magazines, his lemon drops, and his pristine coats. Liked him enough to forgive his misidentification of her symptoms as "psychologically derivative." Liked him enough to agree to volunteer at the city library's Visually Impaired Assistance Program for "purpose and routine."

* * *

On a Monday at 4:28 P.M., Anna knocked on Sam's apartment door. It was the same knock she knocked every week for twelve weeks—like she knew he knew she was already there. Her knee hurt and the building elevator was under renovation, so the two flights of stairs added a glisten to her forehead and a rhythm to her breathing. She hated herself for it. Back when her back could bend and her toes could point, Anna could do Black Swan's thirty-two fouettés en tournant without moistening her leotard—spinning and tucking on a single slipper. Aging is harder for beautiful people, and Anna was beautiful. The *was* haunted her from mirror to mirror in her Westchester high-rise. People used to stare at her, envy her, pay seven dollars to watch her grand jeté at the Metropolitan Opera House. But not Sam. Sam never watched her do anything. So twice a week, Anna didn't watch herself. His place had no mirrors and even his fogged eyes were unreflective. So when he opened his door, she focused on his face.

"Hi Anna," said Sam.

"Hi Sam," said Anna. He reached forward, placing a hand on her elbow in his standard gesture of greeting.

"Your knee doing okay?"

"Well, not really." She stepped forward, swinging the door shut behind her. "They just don't know about these things these days. Might be pulmonary tuberculosis. They just don't know." She shook her head. "There's a large brace on it right now, actually."

There wasn't a large brace on it, actually, but Anna liked the way it sounded. She also liked Sam.

Sam hadn't always been blind; he'd managed a whole two years before the fog came. His visual memory puzzled him, tricked him, disillusioned him. Trapped him with a visual arsenal of table bottoms and grown-ups' feet, forever restricting him from the bipedal perspective. He was a master's student in a divinity school just outside the city, and at night, in the black, he moved about his apartment, tracing his fingers across the thousands of tiny dots of Jacob and Isaiah, Luke and Matthew. Fingering the Psalms and stroking the Gospels. "Religious Studies," he would clarify to friends and uncles and the women like Anna who read to him. "I study God, not worship Him."

Sam's apartment lived an immaculate life. Clutter was more than an inconvenience—it was a hazard. Anna walked by the Bibles and Torahs and Korans convened with books on Indian cooking and music theory in alphabetized rows of Ikea shelving. He'd built them himself. Felt every screw and every piece of artificial wood, sliding them together as Anna read him the instructions during one of her first visits. Everything had a location. Every utensil had its hook and every coat had its hanger. Tiny blue dotted labels speckled the apartment like some kind of laboratory. The microwave buttons, the light switches, the drawers, the cans: all had their names displayed in bright Braille blue. A Malaysian tapestry hung above the sofa and an Andy Warhol print hung opposite the door. "For company," he shrugged when Anna asked. "My mother's idea."

"Well, sit down, sit down!" He gestured to the exact spot of her usual armchair, turned forty-five degrees to the left, and took six paces before stopping in front of the counter. "I've got a lot for you today."

"I think I can handle it," she said.

"Anna, Anna." He mocked distress. "What would I possibly do without you?"

"You know perfectly well they'd just send someone else by."

Sam smiled as he placed his pile on the table.

"I'm teasing you," he said. "You know I love teasing you. Come on, sit down. I don't want that knee of yours giving way. What was it? Pulmonary tuberculosis? Let's not play around with pulmonary tuberculosis."

Anna could see Sam's grin, but she blushed anyway. She sat down and studied him. The way his skin held taut around his forearms, the way his pants creased in as he walked, the way his hands pulled and pushed and shifted and organized, steadily, confidently, free from a seer's incessant second glances or double checks. He was young, and his hair was thick, and his body was still strong. Anna thought he had a dancer's body and imagined his hands on her waist, lifting her up above his head before placing her down as he jumped. She imagined his fingers tracing her fingers in backstage shadows, the pulse of the crowd turning air to endorphin. High off the heat of their bowing bodies, all she could hear was the rhythm of their breath. The same breath she felt quicken when she sat in this armchair, when she slipped off her shoes and sat down to read.

"All right then." Sam handed her the pile of mail and bills and misplaced receipts. "Let's start with the boring stuff." He sat down at his computer, ready to translate her voice into his language of dots.

She read him an advertisement for car insurance and unbuttoned her sweater.

She read him a credit card receipt and rolled down her stockings.

Sam sat at his desk, blind. Sat typing and sipping and small-talking between his chorus of Toss it. Toss it. Keep it. What? Toss it. What? Repeat that. Don't throw that out! Anna knew she wasn't the strongest reader; she'd spent her childhood staring at mirrored music boxes, not pages of books. But he never corrected her. Never smiled into his keyboard when she struggled with *entrepreneur, bureaucracy, Jesuit, psalms*. Not like Martin. Martin would have said something, would have laughed. Laughed at his wife, who—"Oh, did I mention, used to dance at the Met." Excused her dinner-party mispronunciation of *bon appétit* to platefuls of partners at the firm's annual dinner. She'd said it again once they'd served the dessert, deviously looking him in the eye and smiling her victorious smile: "Bone appetite, everyone! Bone appetite!"

But that was before Martin retired. Before he left work to stay home and question the amount of mayonnaise in the tuna salad and why she let that damn Chinese family overcharge her for the dry cleaning. Before he reconsidered and, at seventy-one, went back to the firm. Before she realized that she'd liked when he complained about the mayonnaise and didn't really mind that he was home for lunch.

One morning, Martin made Anna scrambled eggs before she woke up. She didn't say anything when they tasted oddly sweet, but once she found the empty cream carton in the trash, they nearly cramped up laughing. The next weekend, Martin took her golfing for the first time. And later that summer to the city for a show. But he must have missed his keyboard and his meetings and his legal briefings because the following fall he went back to his office, his job, his early mornings and late dinners. Anna's career had peaked in her twenties, deteriorating with her body, not expanding with her mind. She retired at twenty-eight and worked in a dance studio for a while, but she eventually settled into her house and her hobbies. His decision puzzled her. And sooner or later her knee started hurting and her nausea began and she got *The Diagnostic Almanac* and Dr. Limestone prescribed her "purpose and routine."

Sometimes, in the shower, or in the car, or loading the dishwasher, Anna would wonder what would have happened if she had offered to read to Martin. Offered her eyes to cable-box directions and instant-soup instructions, unpaid bills and pages from his law books. *I'll be your glasses,* she would have said. *That doesn't say milk, it says cream.*

* * *

On Wednesday at 4:22 P.M., Anna knocked on Sam's apartment door.

"Hi Anna," said Sam.

"Hi Sam," said Anna. He placed his hand on her elbow.

"Your knee doing okay?"

"Not really, Sam. They think it might be a sign of hemolytic anemia."

"That's terrible, Anna. Come on, sit down, sit down."

She sat.

"I'm just tired. I'm tired all the time. I wake up and I'm tired, I go to sleep and I'm tired." She looked at him; he looked slightly to the left of her.

"You know I love having you here, but there are other volunteers in the program and if you're too—"

"No, please," she interrupted. "Really, I'm fine." Anna brushed past Sam and settled on the sofa. "Did I ever tell you I could do Black Swan's thirty-two fouettés en tournant without breaking a sweat?"

Sam smiled.

"I'll put on some tea." The kettle needed washing and Anna was wearing a dress, so by the time he sat down at his desk, her clothes were already piled neatly beneath the armchair.

He looked at her. She loved when he looked at her. Loved imagining Martin imagining him looking at her. As he sat at his firm's desk, too good to retire, staring at a case as his wife parted her bare legs in the apartment of a younger man.

Anna hadn't made love since Martin un-retired. Or for that matter since her knee started hurting and the nausea began. But her pulse would quicken like it did in her twenties. Sometimes, when she'd finished a sentence, or a letter, she'd pause for a minute, letting Sam's clicking fingers catch up, and close her eyes. Sam couldn't see the way her breasts hung down in pockets of thinning skin. Or the way her pubic hairs had begun to thin near the bottom. So she imagined that they didn't and they hadn't. Anna just sipped her tea and let the years fall off her with her clothes. She was twenty-five. Her skin was taut and her hair strawberry yellow. Her joints were smooth and her voice was crisp.

That morning in her closet Anna sorted through options. Straps were preferable. Cottons and silks were quieter, skirts and dresses easier to remove. Buttons were practically essential. Her knuckles struggled with detail, mandating a patient delicacy in sliding the tiny polished plastic through their knitted holders. She started with a hand on her neck, lingering on the divot above her collarbone before sliding her fingertips under the strap and letting it fall off her shoulder like a leotard. Sentence by sentence, she fingered the circles, tossing them aside with the periods, semicolons, and dots from the *i*'s. Sometimes, though, the anticipation was too much. Sometimes Sam would turn toward her at the right moment and her lips would part, and her back would hurt, and she'd lose her place on the page—looking back at Sam like she'd looked at Brian from Conservatory or Lev from her summer in Moscow or Martin before he'd taken the bar. It was these times that she ached to rip off her straps and to let her buttons crack off like tiny moons.

* * *

"I miss dreaming forwards," Anna said.

"What?"

"I dream backwards now. You won't believe how backwards you'll dream someday." She cupped one of her breasts in her hand, sliding it up her body and closer to her neck.

"I didn't think dreams had directions." His broken eyes managed a smile.

"You're teasing me."

"Anna, I would never tease you," he teased. She liked the way he said her name. It rolled off his tongue to say I'm talking to you, to say I'm listening to you.

"I dream of the past, of things that could have happened, or should have happened or never happened. You dream of the future. You're so young, Sam. You don't realize it now, but you're so young."

"I dream in sounds and tastes and textures," he said.

She paused for a moment, studying his half-lidded eyes.

"Future sounds." She reopened the book. "Future tastes and textures."

* * *

Sam wasn't lonely. Not completely. His mother came up from Jersey every few weeks, and some of his college friends still lived in the city. They'd warned him about enrolling in a "normie" program. His college had been filled with dark classrooms and Braille keyboards, audio books and hallway railings. A college where students left their red-striped canes at the bottom of the staircase, feeling forearms and cupping faces. Pressing together to the vibrations of the speakers, dancing and slipping back to unmade beds based on the smell of someone's hair or the curve of their wrist or the way their breath tasted. From time to time, Sam would sit awake in his living room, drink a Bordeaux, and blast these half-forgotten rap songs. He couldn't stand to have a roommate, to subject some Westchester graduate student to the role of perpetual babysitter. After all, he already had nannies. Women who came and read to him like he was some charity case. But Anna was different. She never asked about his classes or his family or what it was like to be blind. It wasn't about him. She just sat down and read. Read until her voice got dry or her eyes got tired and they would merely sit in silence for a while. She understood silence the way he understood darkness—running from neither as the sun set and the words ran out.

* * *

Sam stayed on his side of the room. He always did. After three weeks, Anna realized his pattern, and with it how easy it was to take off her scarf without notice. How easy it was to do the same with her sweater. Her blouse. Her beige cotton underwear. Three months later the routine had evolved. At around 6:30 P.M. she'd excuse herself to the bathroom, bunch up her pile, and emerge fully clothed and fully satisfied. Even as she sat in her kitchen, Martin-less. More satisfied that she was Martin-less. Itching as she ate her dinner to ask how his arthritis was, how his hemorrhoids were doing, and how very exciting his day was.

One night, as she waited, Anna fantasized about choking to death. Martin would come home from work and find her dead on the kitchen floor, a giant slab of steak still warm in a puddle of watery blood, a single fatal bite missing from its side. Her funeral would probably have a slide show of pictures back from the opera house; perhaps her nephew would read one of his poems. Beef would be banned from all hors d'oeuvres. Didn't you hear, people would whisper, that's how she died. I just can't imagine, they'd sob, died in her own kitchen. Anna wondered whether an article would run in the *Times*, or if she'd just get one of those one-liners in the *Westchester Daily*. Alone, in the evenings, when Martin was at the office and her daughter was living in London and her Portuguese cleaning lady was gone and her Chinese dry cleaner was gone and Sam was somewhere dark, Anna thought about such things. Thought and thought until she felt the satiating company of the guilt she'd inspire and the soothing comfort that surely she'd be missed. But then she'd think more. Think and think until she started cutting her steak into smaller and smaller pieces, overchewing each bite before she tentatively swallowed.

* * *

Anna read Sam a wedding invitation and peeled off her socks.

Anna read Sam a chapter from *The Tao of Pooh* and unclasped her bra.

The heating vent chocked.

The tea percolated.

The clock hit 6:30, and Anna went to the bathroom.

* * *

And so it went. Twice a week, every week, for twelve weeks. Anna bought a book on Malaysian culture and another on Indian cooking and another on the faith of Tao. Martin came home, tired, old, proud. And Anna told him about the dry cleaner and the tuna salad and the similarities between Judeo-Christian monotheism and the singularity of Allah. But Anna was still sick, and she knew it. She told Martin, but he told her she was just bored. That she should just find more things to do with her day. That her knee was fine and the nausea was normal.

That night she went to bed earlier than early and forgot to leave a towel for his bath or water for his pills and lay propped up in bed beside her almanac. She had purposefully climbed in on Martin's side of the bed, pretending to be asleep for a whole thirty minutes before she heard him sigh, walk around the bed, and lower his weight inside the cold half of the sheets. Anna pressed her face into her pillow and scrunched up her features. But Martin was snoring before he could feel the blankets shaking slightly up and down.

* * *

On Tuesday at 7:53 P.M., Anna was fantasizing about choking to death when her phone rang. No one called at this hour. Martin wasn't home yet, so she hoped it wasn't someone trying to sell her something; somehow she could never figure out how to hang up on those people. She let it ring a few times just in case it was Martin dialing in his delay—she never answered right away, never wanted to seem like she was waiting.

She picked up. It was the annoying woman who sat at the front desk of Martin's firm. Occasionally she'd call to say he'd be running late—that there was some meeting or that his car wouldn't start. Anna hated when she called. She had bad taste in Christmas cards and had let herself get fat.

"Anna, hi, is that you?" She paused. Her voice sounded funny.

"Yes it is. Is Martin running late?"

She didn't answer.

"Hello? Sorry, can you hear me?" Anna hated the new phones Martin had installed last summer—she never knew quite where she should be talking into.

"Yes, yes, I can. Anna . . ." She paused again. "They told me I should call you . . . better than the police or something. I . . . I really don't know how to say this. Anna—Martin had a heart attack."

Anna swallowed.

"Where is he? Which hospital? Last time they took him to Pembrook and he had to stay the night. Is he on that machine yet? Let me—" But the woman interrupted her.

"Anna, I don't think you understand. It's not like that this time. He pressed the buzzer and we called 911, but when we got back in there he was . . . they tried . . . Anna, I . . . I'm so sorry. I don't know what to say."

Anna was silent.

"Oh . . . dear . . . I . . . is anyone else home?"

"No."

"Anna . . . they did everything, really."

Silence hung between them for a good ten seconds.

"You have a car, I presume, um, can you get to the hospital?" Anna could feel her throat tightening as the phone began to shake against her face.

"I . . ." Anna swallowed. "I'm not supposed to drive into the city at night." She couldn't think, couldn't breathe.

"All right, um . . ." She heard muffled voices in the background. "We're sending someone. Sit tight, Anna, I . . . I'm so sorry."

Anna hung up the phone and stared at her watery steak. Surely there was some mistake. The desk lady was crazy anyway. Martin would drive home in an hour or two, tired, hungry, and homesick. And Anna would make him eggs and lie next to him in bed and read him his papers or his letters or some entries from her almanac. And he would roll over to her side of the bed and stay there forever. Agree to retire for good this time. And then they'd play golf, and cook, and see a show in the city, and she'd read him the scorecard and recipes and the playbill.

Anna pushed her plate away, looking down then up then ahead, her features scrunched and paralyzed in silence. She lifted up her hands, clenching them slowly together. She stood up, walked into the living room, and then walked back to the kitchen. Martin wasn't dead. He wouldn't just die like that. People don't just die like that. She pulled her steak in front of her, swallowing hunks whole, forcing down bites too large for her esophagus. Swallowed and swallowed and swallowed until it was gone. Until she hadn't choked. Until she couldn't swallow her throat's other lump and let her wrinkled face sink to her hands.

Anna walked over to the phone, dialed Sam's number, and hung up.

* * *

On Wednesday at 4:42 P.M., Anna knocked on Sam's apartment door.

"Hi Anna," said Sam.

Anna looked at him.

"How does your knee feel today?"

"Yes," she said. "Yes, it is."

Anna went inside and sat down.

Sam tilted his head slightly and chuckled.

"No tuberculosis or anemia or endometrial cancer?"

"No," she said. "No, there isn't."

Sam put on some tea and handed her his pile.

"I've got a lot for you today. Two of those Saint Augustine chapters, and I want you to look at this pile of coupons."

She read him an advertisement for car insurance.

She read him a sheet of coupons for Walgreens.

She read him a page of Saint Augustine's philosophy.

Sam's clicking stopped. He looked toward her as if listening for something, or smelling for something or tasting for something or feeling for something.

"Are you okay?" he asked.

Sam stood up from his desk, went into the kitchen briefly, and walked over to her side of the room. Sam never left his side of the room.

"I found this on the chair and I presume it's yours." Sam leaned against her chair, handing her a thin beige cardigan. Anna took it from him, careful to avoid meeting his skin.

"Thank you, Sam. I must have left it here."

Sam wasn't certain if he was looking directly at Anna's eyes. He was never certain with her. He could only guess, wonder, speculate until he told himself he was being silly, being egocentric, being sick.

"Anna," he repeated, reaching out slowly, hesitantly, before placing a hand on her shoulder—exhaling into relaxation as he felt the smooth linen fabric beneath his fingers. "You sure you're okay?"

Anna nodded, knowing he could somehow sense the motion of her head. Then picked up the book, dislodging his hand.

"I'm fine, Sam. Really."

She listened to the sound of the tea percolating and thought about their mutual senses; it smells like cinnamon berries, it tastes like honey smoke, it feels warmer today. "Did I ever tell you I could do Black Swan's thirty-two fouettés en tournant?"

"No." Sam went back over to his desk and resumed his clicking. "You've never told me that, Anna. That's impressive."

Then Anna read to Sam. Read to him as he turned her words into a language of spots. A language that she now knew he could read in the steam and in the tea and in the books and in his body. In the painting and the shelves and the music and the air.

Anna brought her mug to the sink before excusing herself to the bathroom. She didn't let him hear her turn the wrong way—but she knew when she clicked shut the front door that he'd know she'd never be back. Knew because her sagging breasts and varicose veins were covered in cotton. Knew because he could hear her tears spot his book like Braille.

The Ingenue

The biggest fight in my relationship with Danny regards his absurd claim that he invented the popular middle school phenomenon of saying "cha-cha-cha" after each phrase of the Happy Birthday song—an idea his ingenious sixth-grade brain allegedly spawned in a New Jersey Chuck E. Cheese and watched spread across 1993 America with an unprecedented rapidity.

"I started that! Are you kidding me!?" His face was serious now, indignant. "Literally, I started that, ask anyone from Montclair!"

"Danny, you did not start that, that's ridiculous." I was serious now, too. "I'm done talking about this."

"No, no, no. Listen. I don't know why this is so impossible to you. Someone had to start it; someone had to be the first kid to say it. I'm telling you, that was me. Eliot Grossman's birthday party. Ask anyone."

"This is really typical."

"What!?" He put his wineglass down on the table.

"Nothing. Just . . . you *would* think you invented something like that. It's just something you would think." I was searching the cabinets for this bag of Goldfish.

"I can't believe you don't believe me about this. It's really pissing me off."

"I can tell."

"Arrgh! This is *really* pissing me off!" His eyes were frustrated and angry in a way I hadn't seen before, and for some reason it satisfied me. I sat on the couch and opened my laptop.

In years to come he would whisper it at parties as the cake paraded by or mouth it across a restaurant table at a sibling's birthday dinner. Cha-cha-cha, he would provoke. Cha-cha-cha, cha-cha-cha.

There was silence for a while and I knew he was brooding.

"Sometimes I hate you," he said. He let the words hang for a moment and then came over and sat next to me, tousling my head into the pillow and kissing me lightly on each eye.

I only tell this story because it reflects why the Yahtzee was so essential.

* * *

There were six of us. Danny, the bearded Noah, the delicate Eric, the old artistic director, and Olivia, whom I hated. Cape Cod was abandoned but we were up in the artistic director's Provincetown shack for a post-cast-party party. Danny was doing summer stock again and I'd driven up for the final performances. I actually ate a lobster by myself before I got to the theater—picking wet meat out of knuckles as I watched the summer's final families appear from a dune drop-off and bang Boogie Boards against the sides of their cars.

The show was terrible for two reasons: one, that the show was terrible, and two, that it involved a lot of kissing. They giggled together, Danny smiling with his eyes inches from Olivia's—pulling at her belt loop and touching her earlobe, which I'd taught him. I wasn't usually so particular about the girls he kissed onstage but there was something about her I didn't like. It started the moment I saw them enter together onstage—holding hands—something disgusting growing in the back of my stomach. She was masculine almost, like an attractive cross dresser, and her genuine tomboyishness unsettled me.

At the party, she wore an actual T-shirt, not fitted or branded, and a flat-brimmed hat with the name of a New Orleans bait shop in neon orange. She drank a beer from the bottle and teased the boys, who didn't realize they stopped talking whenever she started to tell a story. I'd clicked through her pictures a few times that summer and imagined, on nights when Danny didn't text back, rehearsals that ended in beers and joints on beaches.

"Show her the one with the square penis!" Olivia laughed, and we all lunged up a banisterless staircase. "Ricky's partner is a painter," she explained. "And he has this painting of a square penis."

"It's not that funny." Ricky, the artistic director, was as drunk as the rest of us.

"It is, Rick," said Noah. "It's ingenious."

"Fuck off."

"It actually is!" The house was old and decorated with an enviable authenticity. We wove through rusted signs and relics from the Army-Navy store until we arrived at the painting, where everyone promptly knelt. I stood awkwardly, not sure whether or not I was involved.

"Get out of here." Ricky whacked Eric on the back of the head. "You're not worthy."

"We know," said Danny. "Trust me, we know."

"You're making yourself look stupid in front of your girl-

friend, you know that?" It was a line from the play and everyone died. Olivia literally rolled onto her side and I felt an odd
nostalgia for my high school friends and the days when everyone shared the same world of people. Noah pulled her up and
I noticed the print on her T-shirt for the first time. There was
a dinosaur that appeared to be riding a bike below a REX'S FIX
UPS AND MIX UPS. It looked familiar: I remembered someone
somewhere making a joke about that dinosaur, laughing in
some bar about its tiny hands leaning down toward the bike's
handles. Eventually, Noah and Eric went downstairs to pack a
bowl and I slipped a hand into Danny's pocket, holding him
back as the rest tumbled down.

"Hi," I said.

"Hi." He smiled. "I love you."

"I love you too. Come here." I pulled him into a corner of
the upstairs space and we leaned against a bookcase, pressing
our foreheads together. I hadn't seen him since July and being
together in groups never felt like being together.

"I miss you," I said.

"I know," he said. "I love you." We kissed but I could tell he
wanted to go downstairs.

"You were good tonight, you know that? That part with
the father, your physicality was really spot-on."

"Thanks." We looked at each other. It was a genuine com-
pliment moment and we were on the same team. "I mean, the
play is shit, but thank you."

"It's not."

"It is." We looked at each other again and grinned at the
same time. Danny rarely admitted this type of thing and I was
overcome with affection. I wanted to crawl into something
and lie with our faces touching for as long as it took to feel
like I didn't miss him anymore. I wanted to do this, to tell him

this, to say I wanted to get out of the house and into the car and onto the freeway where we could zoom away from all the attractive people I didn't know, but Danny was looking at me, almost studying me, and took my shoulders in his hands as if surprised.

"Argh, man," he said. "I missed you. I really did miss you." His eyes were sad and he kissed me on the nose. It was as if he'd just realized it. Just actualized the refrain of our phone calls.

"Good," I said. Worried, rather than hurt, that I might have to pull him back in. That he was sad to be heading home to our TV shows and late-night snacks and unmade cave of a bed.

We were so compatible, really. Really just so compatible in a number of ways. We had the same favorite band, the same exact one, and I used to act too, in college. We bonded over this at the party where we first met—some mutual friend of a friend and I had walked into an unlocked bathroom to reveal him rinsing with the apartment owner's Listerine. We'd found this remarkably hilarious and I liked the way he made fun of me while holding eye contact. When we walked back to his place, I told him I had quit theater because it was never my primary focus to begin with and, besides, I was never that good. He said I was probably being modest (Danny always flirted with flattery) and for the first and only time in my life, I made out a good deal on the subway.

"You know the Books are playing in Prospect Park next weekend," I said, my hands still in his pockets. "We should go."

"Yeah, for sure."

"Go to that Vietnamese place before."

"Yeah, totally." We could hear the wind rattling the deck umbrella in its metal holder and I thought for a minute about the vast stretch of beach we couldn't see in the dark—about how the tide could be dead low or dead high and we wouldn't even know. But the thought of Brooklyn had popped the image of Rex's Fix Ups back into my head and I almost said something but decided not to. The shop was on Dean Street. The shirt belonged to Danny.

I heard shouting from the kitchen and it sounded like Olivia was laughing at Eric for spilling some kind of drink.

"I'll kill you!" she shouted. "Hom-o, hom-o!" Chairs seemed to be sliding and we heard something drop. "Hom-o, I'll eat you!" Danny tried not to smile but his face broke and he stifled a laugh.

"I'm sorry," he said, still grinning. "I'm sorry, it's just . . . I'm sorry." He couldn't keep a straight face.

"It's fine," I said, smiling back at him. "It's fine. Let's go."

I kissed him on the cheek and we turned to leave, the umbrella still rattling from outside the glass.

It wasn't until we were walking back down the stairs toward the maze of antiques and squealing actors that I truly realized I despised Olivia and her flat-brimmed hat with an unbearable and irrational intensity.

The next day, I watched the play again. It was a matinee, so the cast scraped out of Ricky's house at eleven o'clock with the pouty camaraderie of a communal hangover. Too tired and confused the night before, Danny and I had had sex that morning—emerging last into the kitchen, secretly superior. I ordered another to-go lobster on the way to the theater and it came with its claws flopping over the sides of a fast food container, which I liked. I sat in the back again but felt a strange sinking when the lights dimmed. Danny looked handsome in his costume: styled, slightly, and forced to wear jeans that fit him.

I don't think I'd ever had a truly violent impulse before that afternoon, sitting in a velvet chair in a dark theater as old people laughed. I had a boyfriend in high school who got into a fight at a party in someone's basement and I remember driving him home in silence, fully incapable of understanding why he felt compelled to punch Joey Carlton in the face for the shit he said about Mike and AJ. But I understood now. Danny and Olivia were just so charming! The part where they first kissed, his hand on the small of her back and her fingers running through his hair. The part where they giggled and eye-smiled and confessed things and fought and made up and cried and kissed again. I wanted to take Olivia's face and hit it as hard as I could. Shove her to the ground and kick her in the side. Smash her against the wall, pull at her hair, punch her again right between the eyes. I imagined doing these things as the audience laughed. Imagined getting up on stage and beating her up. Just literally beating her up. Fuck you, I would say. Fuck you and your stupid clothing and your stupid attitude and the way you talk to everyone like they fucking love you. Stay the fuck away from Danny and if you ever fucking talk to him again I will kill you, I would say. I will literally kill you.

During intermission I went outside to sit in the car because I didn't feel like talking to the lobby and its circles. Part of me probably knew it was coming because as soon as I shut the door, I started crying. I let my head hang forward and press against the steering wheel but after a few sobs I sat up and stopped. I texted five or six friends from the city. Small things like "hey how's work?" or "ugh I want to kill this girl in Dan's play." I do that sometimes when I'm feeling lonely; it's a strange and compulsive habit, but it usually works. I waited for a minute before anyone responded. Flipped down the mirror and rubbed my knuckle under my eyes, exhaling. My sister and my friend Tara texted me back and I responded to both immediately. I spent the second half of the play reminding myself of particular ways in which I was better than Olivia: I was thinner, I had nicer eyes, I went to a better school.

I didn't know what my problem was. Danny had been a (struggling) actor since the day we met and I'd seen him kiss girls onstage before. I guess the summer had been hard; the cell service in northern Cape Cod wasn't great and I'd wonder about him all day as I sat in my office. The envy was twofold: jealousy of the girl he was spending time with and jealousy of how he was spending his time. Playing around all day doing stretches and dumb acting games, getting wasted at night at the Beachcomber, the local bar he raved about whenever we talked on the phone. "It's so fun," he'd say. "There's this group of local alcoholics who are too freaking funny. But they have these bands that come and everyone just sort of goes with it, you know? None of that too-cool bullshit." "Yeah," I'd say, in bed with my salad. "It sounds amazing, you'll have to take me when I come up in August." "For sure," he'd reply. "I can't wait."

We got dinner together between shows and had sex again on these inland dunes. Danny parked the car on the side of Route 6 next to a beach pine marked with an orange plastic flag.

"This way," he said, leading me up a path through scratchy trunks growing sideways out of sand. "I'm telling you, this place is unreal."

It was. We emerged from the cropped forest into an expanse of craters, dune grass waving from the tops of their peaked edges. The sun hadn't quite set but the crickets were pulsing—chirping from the green patches with astonishing volume. It was windy, and strips of hair blew out of my ponytail and across my face. Danny stretched his arms up and leaned forward into the wind.

"Isn't it amazing?"

"Yeah," I said, pulling on a sweatshirt.

"We come here a lot at night." He jumped forward and down in massive leaps, sand sliding in chutes behind him. I leapt after, shrieking, and landed in a heap at the bottom, rolling next to him.

We had the idea at the same moment and kept our clothes on the whole time. When we were done, I lay down beside him and looked up at the thin clouds. I thought about how funny we must look from above—lying in the center of a bowl-shaped hole in the world. I imagined what it would be like if every crater had a couple at its center, looking up.

"Do you ever come here with Olivia?" I asked. Cupping sand in my hands and letting it sift into a pile.

"Sure," he said. "We all come here." I knew my jealousy was unattractive, that Danny would think I was insecure, but I couldn't stop.

"Yeah, but do you come here with just her?"

He rolled over to face me.

"Olivia and I are friends," he said. "We do shit together."

"Like kiss every night."

"Onstage. In a play." I didn't say anything. He sat up. "You're not serious, are you?"

I reverted, pulling my head inside my sweatshirt in mock retreat.

"I hate her!" My voice came out muffled. I popped back out. "I hate her, I hate her." I smiled, and it worked: the intensity of the moment vanished as fast as I'd created it.

We lay there in silence for a while, but it was ruined. I knew the way Danny thought and I knew this only made him like me less and like her more. For the second time that day I wanted to hit something but I still couldn't help myself. I rolled over and kissed at his neck.

"Remember that T-shirt she was wearing yesterday?"

"Who? Olivia?"

"Yeah." I paused. "Did you give it to her? I thought you had that shirt." He sat up again, serious this time. Cupped my hands in my lap.

"Listen," he said, his eyebrows raised. "I love you, okay?"

"I know."

"I don't want to convince you."

"I know," I said. "I'm sorry." The crickets droned and I stood up to shake sand off my back. "I just—love you."

He looked at me and tucked my loose hair behind my ears.

"I love you too," he said. But I never got my answer.

The Yahtzee happened that night. After the play. I went for a third time despite Danny's genuine suggestion that I sit this one out. In the hour beforehand, I walked to the Penny Patch, the old candy store in the village by Wellfleet Harbor. I ate a small piece of chocolate fudge, a small piece of penuche fudge, and three saltwater taffies and decided I was being ridiculous about the whole thing. Danny and I had gone out to dinner. We'd had sex in the bottom of a romantic dune crater. We'd been dating since we were twenty-four. I'd gone to Minnesota with his parents; he'd come to my grandfather's funeral. Olivia was strange and loud and a tomboy and they loved her because she was one of them, drinking beers and wearing dumb hats. Tomorrow I would pack Danny inside my car and we'd zoom off on the freeway and back inside the walls of New York.

The fact that I had to watch it a third time was almost comical. The approach this time ended up as a complex and detailed imagining of exactly what Danny and Olivia did together offstage. Wishing each other luck before their first entrance. Squeezing hands behind thick black curtains on the side of the theater. Rapidly changing costumes at intermission and catching glimpses of each other's underwear.

When the show was over, I acted extremely cool. Involving myself in the standing ovation and congratulating Olivia when she came out the side of the theater. I even winked at Danny, which he thought was funny, or pretended to. The cast and crew were hopped up on nostalgia—and the whole thing felt a lot like the last night of camp. We grouped up in cars and headed to the Beachcomber, where the local alcoholics and bad bands were as prominent as promised. I actually got a bit drunk off gin and tonics and Danny must have been listening at the dunes because he paid a lot of attention to me. The morning hovered over all our actions with a kind of euphoria. I decided I hated Cape Cod as much as I hated its summer heroine, and the hours until I could cross back over its metallic bridge ticked down with each exceedingly dizzy hour.

The six of us ended up at Ricky's just like the night before. Danny, the bearded Noah, the delicate Eric, Olivia, and me. We had to do the whole ordeal with the square penis again, running up the stairs and kneeling before Ricky lumbered up to kick us down. Everything felt very exciting and very immature at the same time and I genuinely fluctuated between resenting my hidden worship of their rural hipsterdom and declaring (internally) that their fun was a little too intentional. Eric forced us into the kitchen, where we were supposed to engage in "slap shots"—a game he insisted was hilarious but involved taking a shot and promptly getting slapped. Ricky didn't understand and the rest of us were too tired for that kind of thing so we ended up sort of loitering and looking in cabinets.

"Game," said Noah, opening and shutting the refrigerator for no reason. "Game!"

"Yes!" Olivia agreed. And it was settled. Danny and Noah went to set something up and Ricky pulled Eric out to clear the table and assemble some kind of smoking situation. I went to place my wineglass in the sink but stopped when I realized Olivia was still standing there and we were alone together for the first time. I looked at her.

"Do you want another drink?" she asked, casual.

"No thank you," I said. Still standing in place. It was silent, awkward.

"Did you like that wine?" she said finally, twisting a ring.

"It was fine."

"Really? I thought it was kind of sweet." We looked at each other for a beat and I walked over to the sink to place my glass in its wet bottom.

"Here," she said, and I placed hers next to mine. It was all very intentional, very clean. And I knew in that instant that Olivia cared deeply about Danny, or she would have left the room. I'd been watching her all weekend but I realized she'd been watching me too. The understanding was empowering.

"You were very good in the play, you know." We circled. "Your physicality was really spot-on."

"Thank you," she said. "Danny told me you used to act."

"I did, yes. It just wasn't that fulfilling in the end. I needed something more . . . permanent. That's not the right word." We looked at each other again and Olivia's face broke into a massive smile. The fullest smile I'd seen her make all weekend.

"What?" I'd been going for condescension.

"Nothing. Just—there's a lot of Danny in you. The way you

talk. Your expressions." For some reason it felt like an insult and I had the desire to smash her face into a wall again. "I mean, you were probably smart to do something else. It's stupidly hard, especially these days. And let's be honest, none of us would be up here if we were actually going to make it." It was a strange thing to say.

"Danny's going to." My response was immediate. "I know Danny's going to."

I'd surprised her. She looked at me sideways because she could tell that I meant it. "I mean, he's really talented, don't you think?"

"Of course," she said. Still trying to figure me out. "He's fantastic."

"Isn't he?"

I smiled. And it seemed like things were shifting. Danny was on my team all along, he had to be, and looking for proof was not the point. Maybe it was the wine or the exhaustion, but for some reason I believed in Danny in that moment like I'd never believed in him before. I raised my eyebrows and left the kitchen.

When we came out, they were setting up Yahtzee. Eric had taken out the pieces and Ricky was scrambling around for pens. Noah was rolling a spliff.

"You know when I was in Taiwan, those monks I was staying with played this game like all the time where they had these dice and these cups and I never really understood how it all worked but they would bet all this crazy shit, like bags of rice or like chickens," he said, licking the joint as he rotated it between his fingers.

"Dude, you gotta stop talking about Taiwan. You're becoming the kid who went to India." Danny tore off a score-card and placed it in front of him.

"I didn't go to India."

"That's not the point." He looked toward Olivia and they shared a smile.

"Noah spent last summer in Taiwan," she said to me. "If you're lucky, he'll show you his album of eight million photographs later . . . but it will be hard because you can't *really* understand unless you've been there."

"Oh fuck all of you," Noah said. He'd finished rolling and everyone was finally gathered around the table.

"Here," Olivia said, pulling a chair back for me. I sat down but I didn't like that she was talking to me now like we were friends.

We started playing. Things began slowly but sped up as we sobered. Apparently their late nights often ended in a game, and their strategies for when to count a three of a kind were beyond me. It was competitive. Danny, Olivia, and Nick were peering over at each other's scorecards and keeping track of who was on track for the thirty-five-point bonus.

"Fives, fives, fives," Noah chanted, using his palm to cover the top of the red plastic cup and shaking. He spilled and we stared. He got a single five and scooped the rest of the dice back to roll again.

"Fives, fives, fives!" He got another five.

"I'm literally going to kill you if you do that every time you roll," Danny said.

"But it works!"

"Fuck off."

He rolled a third time to reveal two more fives and stood up to high-five Eric. "Aye yi yi! Five-sa fives!" Danny swiped up the dice for his turn and ended up a lucky but last-minute small straight. Still, he was losing and he didn't like it.

The game meandered on and stories began to take over.

It was getting late but going to bed meant good-bye so we pushed forward. My anger had begun to fade to apathy as the prospect of tomorrow loomed nearer and I could get in the car and be done with the whole ordeal.

But that's when I saw it happen. Noah was telling a story about a production of *Othello* in this Queens warehouse where a castmate filled his water-glass prop with vodka as a prank before he walked onstage, forcing him to take small shots throughout his climactic scene with Emilia. Ricky was eating it up and everyone watched him as he mimed his narration with his whiskey and Coke. Even I was laughing, but I turned an eye toward Danny as he finished his last turn. If it had been a second earlier or a second later I would have missed it, but for some reason I looked back at him at that moment and saw his hand dart up toward the table and switch a two to a four. Just like that: rotating the die on its side and sliding his hand back to his lap. It was subtle. Quick. But it said everything. Absolutely, absolutely everything.

"Yahtzee!" he shouted. Standing up and grinning right at Noah. "Yaht-zeeee!"

"Bastard," Noah said.

"Dannyyy," Olivia whined.

"He always wins." Eric took a final hit off the joint. "You suck."

Danny beamed and moved his shoulders side to side in a little dance.

But everything was so instantly, remarkably different. I was shocked. Literally incapable of comprehending what I'd seen. I felt stabbed, like the air was forced out of my chest, and I looked at him aghast, hurt, shut behind walls. It was unfathomable to me. The game didn't matter. The stakes were so low. There was no part of me that would—could—ever consider doing what he did. But it was so easy for him. The easiest thing. And that, I realized, had been there all along.

I've wondered sometimes if things would have turned out differently if I hadn't seen him turn the die. If I'd lingered a few more seconds on Noah's bearded laugh or taken a sip of my drink. Or if I'd chosen to say something. Stand up, wide-eyed, and make the public accusation. Embarrass him, force him to grovel in front of his darling and her cohorts.

But the articulation of his crime would have been meaningless; he would never have understood just how deeply that tiny turn of his wrist had pierced me. Just how utterly I'd been reduced. Mocked. Betrayed.

I didn't say much for the rest of the night. Sat stiff in my chair and even stiller in our bed when he stroked me. He asked me if something was wrong just before we fell asleep but it didn't seem worth it.

"Are you still upset about Olivia?" I nearly laughed. Olivia was nothing, I wanted to say. It was a carnival. That's all.

I woke up at sunrise to a dead-low tide, placed my skirts and flats in neat piles inside my bag, padded down the staircase, and walked out the door into the now crisp Cape Cod air. The drive to New York felt short and I didn't stop until I reached the city and walked in the door and padded up the staircase and turned off my phone to sleep for a long, long time.

* * *

I remember trying to explain to my mother why the Yahtzee was so essential but she didn't understand. We were getting lunch on Bleecker and I was trying to convince her I was doing *okay*. She'd driven up from Pennsylvania but all I let us talk about was my sister's sister-in-law and the Oscar nominations. It was pouring rain but it stopped by the time she paid the check and the restaurant's awning dripped outside the window. We had plans to spend the afternoon at the Met but the prospect seemed unbearably exhausting. I imagined myself holding a brochure and walking from room to gigantic room with waning focus. I'd read descriptions on marble walls and realize I'd stopped comprehending. I'd begin to look for benches. I'd become dehydrated. Outside, the sun would blare and crowds of people would wait, sunburned, to get inside. I'd want to go home and sink into bed or at least sit down for more than two minutes. But I wouldn't be able to. And it would hurt me. Frustrate me. The waiter came back to pick up the check and a cupcake passed by with a sparkler candle flicking.

Cha-cha-cha, I thought. Cha-cha-cha, cha-cha-cha.

In years to come he would whisper it at parties as the cake paraded by or mouth it across a restaurant table at a sibling's birthday dinner. On our wedding night, Danny winked at me when the cake came out and we both knew what he was thinking. My mother always said how amazing it is that things seem so absolute when you're young. But the sand slides down in chutes until the dune craters are all full. Inevitable, the magazines write, and we shake our heads with somber nostalgia for the grass and its crickets. We always will.

The Emerald City

To: Laura.Kenzie@gmail.com
From: William.Madar@CPA.Kellogg.gov
Date: Jun 16, 2003 at 10:56 PM
Subject: melting! (the Green Zone hit 108°)

Laura darling,

I stopped carrying my gun today. To be honest, we
don't really need them. It's like we're all inventing our
adventure—crawling through the Baghdad gardens like
the seeds are mines, like the bruised pears might blow our
damn legs off. Wolf still carries his M-9 on the boulevard,
belting it to cargos like his comic book idols. (The nerds
in the Coalition Provisional Authority are keen on the war
glory stuff.) I'm no wannabe soldier, though; I don't have
to tell you that. Not joining the Army is just about the best
decision I ever made. I stopped romanticizing this place
long before the juniper trees blossomed and they reopened
the Green Zone swimming pool. I eat Afghan bananas in
an office in a palace in a peace zone for God's sake. Outside,
it's just a bunch of bodies slamming against stones, lurking
in desert hidey-holes until their human fuses explode.

I've been thinking a lot about you, if that means anything.
There's this river here, Laura, this river that bends through
the irony of Saddam's old statues and monuments and
other marble tyrannies. The Arabs call it "Dijla" but every
Bible reader east of Persia knows it's the Tigris—pouring
through the sand straight from Mesopotamia. Probably the
first thing to get a name when Civilization started pointing
and writing. Well when it's hot and the guards don't have
a captain around, they let some of us down to sit on the
blast walls by its bank. Wolf and Michael bring beers and
laugh about the Texans or talk about college. But when
I look at water, I think of New Hampshire. The way you
smelled like blueberries and pine when we'd sit on that
dock.

I'm so self-indulgent, Laura! But I suppose you're used
to forgiving my poetry. God knows the soldiers would
crack up if they read this. It's funny enough that a skinny
architect ended up redistricting Iraq. But it's nice doing
something that (theoretically) helps the world. I was sick of
designing parking lots and industrial boringness. But you
know that.

Truth is I don't know what to say, really. The Green Zone's
hardly exciting these days, especially not for us civilian
office slaves contracting for the CPA. Perhaps I should just
pretend to be your lost lieutenant, sniping terrorists with
your picture at my breast.

Mostly, we just battle time. Sweating through zip-off pants
and moving like moths to the air-conditioned pockets of
this place. They finally moved my department out of the
hotel offices and inside occupation headquarters in Saddam's
old palace. (Now it's all diplomats and policy snobs.) I'm

still living in that trailer, though. But despite the heat, it's not so bad. I've set up this shelf and managed to buy a coffee maker off a friend who works in the kitchen. There's a Pleasantville quality about it all—the matching trailers lined up with manicured grass and palm trees. Even the roads are surreal—Hummers driving at slow-motion speed, obeying the zone's 35 mph cap.

My work's the same. I've officially been promoted to Deputy Secretary of Housing Reconstruction and Redistribution, but titles don't mean much around here. I'll finally have my own translator though (thank God). I think the Iraqis are starting to realize the permanence of things. Last week, Wolf and I checked on the Shi'as we moved into one of the In-Zone complexes and hardly any families had unpacked. This woman boiled chickpeas on a suitcase counter, forbidding her children to unzip their duffel bags. She was just stirring this pot, stirring and stirring and shaking her head. Wolf gave the kids Tootsie Rolls, but she threw them back at him. I looked her file up later and it said her husband died in the bombing.

These people don't get it, Laura. They don't get that our trailers won't leave come September. Then again, I'm not sure the CPA really gets this either. I'm starting to think we're here for the long run. Which is hard when I tend to garrulous musings on blueberries and pine.

Look, Laura, I'm sorry if this is weird. I know we said we'd leave things ambiguous—but when you didn't show up at my good-bye party, I wasn't sure what to think. If you want me to stop writing, I will. Really, I will. Just know that I'm thinking about you. Know you're my tether outside these walls.

Is Manhattan hot? Have the Japanese invaded or is it still too early in the summer? I'd tell you more about this strange country if I could, but I'm caged up. They've built us this greenhouse and won't let us out.

Anyway, my fan died, so I should probably sleep before I melt. I swear this whole desert's going to melt into glass by August. But don't worry about me, Laura, really don't. It's safer than the city in here, I promise.

Your long lost soldier CPA officer, Will

* * *

To: Laura.Kenzie@gmail.com
From: William.Madar@CPA.Kellogg.gov
Date: Jun 24, 2003 at 12:39 PM
Subject: greetings from kebab-land

Laura!

I'm eating a kebab right now and it's raining outside. This juxtaposition is just about the best thing to happen all month. CPA turned the palace ballroom into a chow hall, so I'm writing to you from quite the elegant milieu. My romanticism pees itself in places like this—you know how I get around high ceilings. I picture Saddam and his sons roaming the naves at some dance. Perhaps stopping at this very spot to smooth out a beard or straighten a robe. We joke that the ghosts of Husseins haunt the hallways at night, creeping out once they lock the marble doors at nine.

I'm in a great mood, Laura. Perhaps the best since I arrived. I was worried when you didn't reply last week that you weren't going to, so when I saw your name in my inbox this morning, I was ecstatic. I know you said not to talk about it, but I'm glad we're staying in contact like this. I miss you, and having someone on the outside is more important than you can imagine.

There's other good news: they assigned me my translator last week and I finally feel like I'll be able to get some work done. Relocating Iraqi families is hard enough without memorized Arabic phrases and awkward insertions of ana asif, ana asif, I'm sorry, I'm sorry.

Her name's Haaya and she's amazing. Her dad was an official of the Iraqi Ba'ath party in the 80's, but her mom's "a soviet." When she was twelve, government men killed her father and brothers while she watched from upstairs—punishment for siding with Kuwait. After that she lived in Russia—but two months out of Moscow University and she's back in the desert—whispering English into turban-less ears.

She doesn't wear a hijab or burka or even long sleeves. She just glides through the palms like she grew them, moves through the palace like it's hers. I didn't even know how much I needed her until she appeared. I can speak now. I can hear now. I can talk to the slum men and the landlords and the vendors selling pita—hear their housing concerns without consulting ten dictionaries. It's just nice having someone to talk to outside the confines of my keyboard. Wolf and Michael are great, but they know more about post-conflict reconstruction policy than anything else (except maybe combat video games).

Haaya studied art history, so we indulge in humanities stuff together. She explained about the buildings and statues and I explained about the designs. Did you know that before the Ottomans, mosques had no ceilings? I like that. It seems more natural to pray in the open air. Haaya prays five times a day despite her bare arms. She has this little mat in her backpack and just excuses herself from meetings. Last night we went to the orange trees and watched the Helipad landings. (She knows the guard who minds the orchard.) I told her about you while we peeled citrus rinds. You'd like each other, I think.

Arghgfljshdfg, Laura! There are so many places I still want to go, so many things I still want to do! Leaving the world of corporations and nine-to-fives has inspired this sort of naïve expeditionism in me. (My computer's telling me that's not a word, but I swear it is.) Have you ever been to Asia? I think we should go to Asia. Asia or Africa. Remember when we used to talk about going on a trip? It was a while ago, but still. I know we agreed not to talk about the future, but they're going to let us out of here eventually. Maybe the US will invade India and we can eat kebabs in their castles. :)

In a strange way, I feel guilty being cheerful. Look at me, eating fruit as I watch the soldiers land and walk single file from their high school hallways to concrete labyrinths and exploding highways. (I know we didn't look that young at 19.) There's a rumor around here that GIs have been leaving their trackers in trashcans while they sleep away their duty parked in fields. The army's a mess and the government knows it. The CPA's trying to do as much as we can via remote control—peering over the Green Zone walls. Haaya was the one who got me thinking. Realizing that our impact could double if they'd actually let us see Iraq.

Oh God, the CPA leadership must have mastered telepathy—Paul Bremer is walking over with his lunch. (You've probably read about it in the news, but he's been top dog around here since May.) Time to pretend I'm analyzing zoning plans! Take care! I miss you! Tell me more about your job, Laura, your last message was so short!

Thinking of you,

Will

* * *

To: Laura.Kenzie@gmail.com
From: William.Madar@CPA.Kellogg.gov
Date: July 5, 2003 at 1:12 AM
Subject:

Laura!!

Happy Fourth of July! I'm juts home now from the green zone party! It was so American but I loved it so much because it love this country so much, I really do. They had it at the swimming poot to raise morale or something and Haaya taght me to Muslim dance, but I cant remember the name of it! It's so hot again, everyone young was swimming all day and they shipped in barbeuqe which made me think of home. I have to tell you Laura I love our country I do. I know we mess up invading and every thing but we are just a bunch of guys trying to share democracy around the world is all it comes down to. You don't see americns blowing up planes do yoU?!? Look, I love you so much Laura I know I'm not suppost to say that but I thought about you and don't worry really I'm ok here, very safe etc.

You should have heard the air force singing the national anthem . . . that's how it should be sung, I know it. This one man—he started crying when he heard it, this one old man who had all the badges from Vietnam he started crying when he heard that cong.

I'm so sleepy I'm about to sleep literally but I thought to send this so you know I'm thinking about you. Write me back I read your letters a hundred timse when you write me back.

Will

* * *

To: Laura.Kenzie@gmail.com
From: William.Madar@CPA.Kellogg.gov
Date: July 19, 2003 at 10:23 PM
Subject: last two weeks

Laura—

I'm sorry I didn't write you sooner but things have been crazy around here. I'm sure you've seen it all on the news (the media's eating it up) but I'll tell you the story sans public opinion concerns. The insurgent truck crashed through the defense and into the Canal Hotel at around 4:30. I was outside (about a half mile away) but every window on Yafa Street shattered in unison. Everyone heard it. I guess curiosity killed precaution because the streets started flowing with smoky, squinting eyes. It's messed up, but people were relieved when they found out it was only UN headquarters. 22 are dead but they got it wrong about the wounded—more like 200 than CNN's 125. With their High Commissioner for Human Rights (ironically) suffocated in rubble—rumor has it that the UN's going to be out of here by August. I wouldn't be surprised.

I started carrying my gun again. It's stupid, but I do it anyway. There was this woman, Laura, and her arm was literally hanging to her body. She was supporting it with her other hand and just walking. Walking away from the hotel, wide-eyed and stricken dumb. She was walking, Laura! Not running, not screaming, just pacing her way down Yafa like the slow-moving cars. I go to sleep seeing that woman's arm and then I wake up and strap my M-9 to my belt. Deep down I know I'm just being stupid. It's not like a gun can stop a car from blowing up.

Everyone's on edge. I caught Wolf reading the CPA safety booklet at lunch and Michael keeps jerking his head into stillness like he's heard some unheard bomb. Haaya's the only one who seems unfazed. ("This is a war.") We've been spending more time in fieldwork and less time in the office. We finally finished screening and documenting the peasants who poured into the Green Zone apartments in the aftermath of occupation. Groups of fourteen and fifteen are crammed into two-bedroom units, but in-zone space is sacred compared to the slums outside the walls. Problem is, now everyone's suspicious of anyone and everyone whose skin isn't pale. The new housing we've been fixing was ready for move-in the day of the crash—but Bremer pushed us back three weeks. It's probably for the best, anyway. People are teeming to get inside the walls and background checks have half the office with headaches.

There's more bad news. Reports of Sunni massacres have started leaking in via civilian slums. Apparently the Iraqi police are behind it. (DO NOT share this information with anyone.) This is why we need to redistrict! If we concentrate the Sunnis we can get the GIs into effective patrols—the CPA notion that desegregation will "address the crisis at its roots" is an ignorant pipedream. This isn't goddamn Jim Crow, it's 1400 years of holy war! It's Sunni men, pillowcased and shot by the Tigris at four am! The Iraqi police patrol by day and ride with the Mahdi army once they finish evening prayer. With access to residence rolls by block, their work is practically done for them— (even I can tell Sunni from Shi'a by last name).

Haaya and I watched the helipad again last night. The orange groves behind the palace have become a routine for us. The days are starting to blend together and it's these moments that get me out of bed. The winds come at night and if we focus we can smell salt from the Caspian. Haaya's been teaching me Arabic. Burtuqal, orange. Nakhla, palm tree. Jundi cheb, boy soldier. Every night, more and more troops fly in and ship out. We watch the lines and line up our peels on the grass. She told me about her family's death for real on Wednesday and I told her about Kyle's overdose and the time I almost dropped out of school. Companionship is everything, Laura. (The heat seems to foster clichés, but it's true.) Wolf and Michael started bunking together, they don't talk much, but they play those combat games on their laptops when they can't sleep.

I miss New Hampshire, Laura. Real trees and fish and hammock chairs. How's the city? Have you seen Shakespeare in the Park yet? I tried to explain this to Haaya by comparing it to pre-Ottoman mosques. I wish you'd tell me more in your messages. Hearing from you really breaks up my day.

—Will

* * *

To: Laura.Kenzie@gmail.com
From: William.Madar@CPA.Kellogg.gov
Date: Aug 2, 2003 at 1:11 AM
Subject: hello

We got news from outside today. (A CPA officer got
authorized to meet with an imam who couldn't come inside
the Zone.) He was walking down a crowded sidewalk in
the central city when an old man carrying two bags of
groceries was accosted by a young guy, demanding his
food and money at knife-point. Pedestrians stopped to
watch, regarding the interaction with normalcy. The old
man reached into his pocket, but instead of withdrawing
his wallet, he took out his gun, switched off the safety, and
shot the man straight in the chest. Some of the pedestrians
cheered, others spat, and the old man picked up his
groceries and continued home. There's Iraq for you.

Haaya suggested we work separately today. I had office
work to do and she wanted to speak to some men in the
slums outside the new housing. I told her I didn't think
it was a good idea, but she insisted. I've been a mess all
day—distracted, exhausted (writing e-mails when I should
be working). I suppose I've come to rely on her more than I
thought.

I know it's been a while since I've written, but I did get
your other messages and I'm sorry I didn't respond sooner.
It's hard to turn my thoughts into words these days. (For
once you don't have to forgive me my poetic verbosity.) But
the beauty of this place is haunting me now. The date palms

bloomed and everything seems overgrown and excessively lush. No one's been contracted to trim the palace gardens or wildflowers, so the greens by the blast walls and rivers are (beautifully) unkempt. But we hear firefights now. Firefights and sirens and tiny pops from the city. The city I've lived in for months but never really seen.

How's work?

* * *

To: Laura.Kenzie@gmail.com
From: William.Madar@CPA.Kellogg.gov
Date: Aug 10, 2003 at 12:35 AM
Subject: hi!

Laura,

Again, sorry it's been so long. My work is starting to consume me and when Haaya and I aren't in the office, we're usually asleep. Finding these moments alone with my laptop is getting harder.

Mostly I've been distracted by the news on the Sunnis. The buzz about the massacres is all over the Zone. It's practically common knowledge that Iraqi police forces are behind the operations—but the CPA is still unwilling to acknowledge that the men they're training are doubling as Mahdi executioners at night. I spent three evenings in a row combing newspapers, but not even the liberals are editorializing about it yet. Haaya thinks the CPA simply doesn't give a shit. Honestly, I wouldn't be surprised if it was true.

Personally, that mindset disgusts me. We have the GIs patrolling, we just need to start stationing them at checkpoints so trucks full of civilians don't get carted off and shot in the mountains. It's not that hard!!! We're talking about sixty people a week, Laura! This isn't some token shooting or car bomb.

There's this man who's started standing outside the palace every day. An old guy, leathered and yellow eyed. He barrages the staff as we walk up the marble steps, screaming for his dead Sunni family and praying in desperate repetitions. Everyone in the office calls him the "crazy sheikh," but no one seems to know whose department is responsible for dealing with it. We just walk by. Walk by with our bush hats and M-9's to push paper in this damn castle.

Haaya and I have been trying to gather some information when we do our housing rounds. We figure if we can get enough legitimate sources maybe someone in the press corps will pick it up and do a story. According to a woman in the market, the Mahdis are starting to take children. Now I picture a kid's head getting blown off every time I hear one of the tiny pops outside the walls. I didn't come here for this, Laura. I thought I'd be making a contribution. I thought I'd be helping the world, not ignoring it.

I'm exhausted. I'm sorry I didn't have time to write something beautiful for you. I bet New York's a dream right now. August was always my favorite month in the city.

Hang in there. Will

* * *

To: Laura.Kenzie@gmail.com
From: SoccerStar73@aol.com
Date: Aug 16, 2003 at 1:06 AM
Subject: delete this when you're done

I'm sending this to you from my childhood address—as the CPA can read our company accounts.

I have news. Haaya has a plan to curb the district targeting of Sunnis but it's not exactly on policy (hence soccerstar73). When we worked alone last week, she met a slum man who got talking about the Mahdis. He knew about the massacres— and claimed to know about the men. When she came back around sunset, she seemed obsessed with the man; the smoothness of his voice, the green of his eyes. He told her they couldn't talk on the street and brought her into the back room of a café on Yafa. (There's no denying her nerve.)

She told me he knows about art, about music, about the irony of the architecture gilding the walls. A university man living in the slums was suspicious to me, but to Haaya, he was a martyr. They ate mangoes and talked every day for five days. Each day I insisted on coming and each day she forbade me to come. (She was trying to gain his confidence, his Arabic was too thick to translate, a foreigner could give "the wrong impression.") I was suspicious, but I trust Haaya, and Haaya trusts him. Apparently, he knows which men in the Iraqi army are involved with the Mahdis. Apparently, he could make a list of them if he had to. A list, Haaya repeated to me as we stretched out beneath our fruit trees. Trust me, she said. Trust me.

I had to. Haaya knows the language and the culture better than I do and we're talking about ten to twenty casualties per night. The deal is this: he wants In-Zone housing for his extended family—the waitlists are huge and even so, he doesn't think they'll pass the background check. Haaya paused when she told me this next part—making sure I was looking in her eyes. His brother used to be affiliated with Al Qaeda—but after 9/11 he pulled back to pockets of moderate Islamists, shameful, confused, and scared shitless. Ta'ib, Ta'ib, he repeated. Reform, Reform, my brother's reformed. I imagine Haaya has sympathy for such men. (Her own father retreated from the Iraqi Ba'ath party during the First Gulf War.)

CPA policy obviously forbids Al Qaeda affiliates (reformed or not) from setting up shop inside the Green Zone Walls—let alone cutting the line of hundreds of translators, embassy workers, journalists, and doctors. Haaya talked of utilitarianism during her pitch. Talked of saving hundreds of Sunni lives, expediting withdrawal, reforming the districts and Iraqi police from within. How many names, I kept repeating. (More for myself than to hear the answer.) Fifty names. Fifty undercover Mahdi names. I counted fifty men, one by one, as they took form, lining the Helipad's east rim. Then I counted fifty men marching to the overnight base, packed inside the inflated dome where they'd sweat through their camo and write home to their moms.

I agreed to do it. My department runs the files on backgrounds and waitlists, and, well, I run my department. Mr. Abdul Aziz Makin will hand Haaya a list of fifty names, which we'll verify before returning with his residency papers. I'm nervous, Laura. But if this works, we have the potential to save thousands of lives. Besides, practically every Shi'a in Baghdad has some sort of former affiliation with Al Qaeda, so it's not like we're actually making some huge exception here. Every time I hear a gunshot from the city I'm more and more assured that this is the right thing to do. Once we clear the Mahdis out of the police, we might finally be able to make some progress in this wasteland.

I've started praying. I'm sure your raging atheism finds this amusing. It's something about this place. The flowers, the marble, the people who don't go more than four hours without stretching towards Mecca. I don't know what God my mind keeps consulting—but I'm hoping it's one who doesn't believe in Jihad.

I still think of you. I know I seem distracted, but it's true. I don't know why you haven't written me in a while, Laura, but I'm guessing you're probably just busy with work or your friends. Let me know how you are.

Your lost soldier CPA officer,

W

* * *

To: Laura.Kenzie@gmail.com
From: SoccerStar73@aol.com
Date: Aug 23, 2003 at 1:25 AM
Subject: delete when done

Laura! I don't want to jinx it but (miraculously) things seem to have worked. We verified the names and the Makins are moving in Monday. Haaya and I are meeting in an hour to decide how to present the list to Bremer and the In-Zone GI unit. Keep your eyes peeled on the papers. This could break soon.

Will

* * *

To: Laura.Kenzie@gmail.com
From: SoccerStar73@aol.com
Date: Aug 27, 2003 at 2:14 PM
Subject: the attack

I'm fine. Turn off the coverage—I don't want you panicking. The Green Zone's been mortared and the Rashid Hotel might collapse under the weight. The first car bomb is linked to the new housing unit and they're calling me in for questioning. Wolf's dead.

I'm freaking out, Laura. If this traces back to our guy it could be bad. I'm just hoping to God that car belonged to some other fucker in the complex. I don't know how I'd live with myself.

Might not be able to write for a while. Delete this.

Will

* * *

To: Laura.Kenzie@gmail.com
From: SoccerStar73@aol.com
Date: Aug 31, 2003 at 2:56 AM
Subject: the attack

Laura,

Haaya wants to leave right now but I told her I needed to do this. I owe you that much. I know it's tactless to do it like this, but there isn't much time so I'm just going to explain everything. They linked the attack to Abdul Aziz and his brother, traced back his authorization papers and found the holes. We explained about the names but it didn't matter—he had the goddamn President on conference. The attack was bad. I'm sure you read about it. Three projectiles to the hotel high-rise and five strategic car bombs in forty-five minutes. The city riots didn't start until the Chinook helicopter got shot down and we lost the Black Hawk. This war is fucked. It's like the country is unraveling from the inside. A bomb aimed at the helipad fell 100m short—falling on the orange groves behind the palace. Unlike the palms, the trees ignited, burning our orchard to the ground and sending citrus smoke through the city.

They're kicking us out. Bremer's giving us two days and our flights leave tomorrow. They didn't explain much but it might be conspiring, if we're lucky just negligence. Either way, we're looking at twenty years minimum. At least they're respecting our dignity with the two days—that and not trailing us with guards until then.

Laura, there's a lot I need to tell you. Haaya and I have made our decision. We're going to leave. An explosion left a hole in the blast wall on the southwest bank that she doesn't think the CPA's noticed yet. If we can get through that, and across the Tigris, she thinks we'll be able to make it to Syria and into the East where she has family. Either way, the walls are closing, and I'd rather be in the desert than a metal box.

The whole Zone's heard it's the "housing guy's fault." I ran into Michael on the boulevard and he just shook his head.

He muttered some bullshit about my Arab girlfriend. He said he thought I was against the war glory stuff. Thought I was better than wanting 50 Mahdis to my name. I didn't even know what to say. It's like something disgusting is rotting in my stomach and I can't get it out. These people are dead because of me. WOLF is dead because of me. I can't stop thinking about the last time I saw him—reading a comic book in the mess hall and offering me the rest of his cantaloupe. I buried the book he lent me by the date plum trees; it's not much, but at least it's something. He was a fucking kid. 23 years old for God's sake.

Haaya tried to take full blame for it—but Bremer was having none of it. He's right. I agreed. I shouldn't have, but I did. I don't know why it matters so much to me, but I want you to know that our intentions were always in the right place. If anything happens to us, at least know that.

Laura, I don't know why you haven't written in a while. I don't even remember when your messages stopped. After the 4th of July? The first attack? I suppose it doesn't matter now. I know you're listening, at least, and there's something in that. I need for you to forgive me. Forgive me for what I did and for what I'm going to do. I can't explain why it matters so much to me, but it does. You were my tether outside these walls, Laura. Always know that.

Haaya and I are going to try to start over. She wants me to pray more—maybe even five times a day. She says the land in the East is barely patrolled, barely settled. And in a few years, I'm sure they'll forget about a CPA fuckup and his translator anyway. Haaya has a headscarf now and she told me to put on dishdasha robes. We'll live with her family for a time. They're farming people, pulling whatever they can from the desert dust.

I'm going to see the world, Laura. I'm finally getting out of this damn garden.

Take care of yourself,

Will

Baggage Claim

Kyle dry-swallowed two aspirin as he entered the warehouse. It reminded him of a Walmart, only larger and more fluorescent. Mellow music hovered over the chatter that only 20 to 30 percent off could possibly inspire. It wasn't his idea to go to the Unclaimed Baggage Center, or, as the women in the matching red polos at the door said, "The Lost Luggage Capital of the World." The building boasted a solid fifty thousand square feet and stretched out like a giant cinder block, awkwardly planted on an island of asphalt in the middle of rural Scottsboro. Bridget had charted this visit into their itinerary long before they had left for Alabama and Kyle had decided he wouldn't like it long before they arrived.

* * *

"Did you know," she had said in the car, "that over one million lost bags come through there every year?" He grunted and looked back at the map. "It says here that one man found an original Salvador Dalí print in an old suitcase." He wondered if she had planned their vacation so he'd finally propose. Wondered if she could sense the ring he had hidden in the cloth in the box in his Dopp kit in the second-smallest pocket of his backpack. Wondered why this somehow annoyed him, and why after all this time *she* somehow annoyed him. The way the foam collected on the corners of her mouth when she brushed her teeth, the way her clothes were always folded in squares, the way she eyed him when he didn't eat his green beans. He didn't bother asking what an "original" print was. Instead he faked a smile, squeezed her arm, and turned off at Exit 62.

* * *

Bridget stared up at the aisle signs hanging from the warehouse ceiling. "The deals here are going to be unbelievable." She did a semicircle, stopping in front of him so their noses nearly touched. "I'm going to go look at those scarves." She kissed him lightly and he noticed her cheeks were sunburned. Kyle nodded as she hurried toward a rack.

Despite the aspirin, a dull headache began to settle in on him. Supermarkets had the same effect—a type of pressure from the plaster above and the linoleum below. He moved down the aisle and emerged in front of a display of digital cameras. Atop the stack was a white-and-red sign proclaiming that ALL PREVIOUS PICTURES HAVE BEEN DELETED FROM THE CAMERAS, and below it was a yellow tag reading TWO-FOR-ONE SPECIAL! Kyle wondered whose job it was to erase the memories from someone else's life. Some young guy who spent his days flipping through the pictures of an Indian couple at a ski resort or a family vacationing in Buenos Aires, monotonously deleting them one after another, perhaps pondering his own means of escaping Scottsboro, Alabama, and his job at its main attraction. It reminded him of a horror movie he had watched with Bridget on one of their first dates. A man received an eye transplant and began to see things from the donor's life. These cameras, he decided, must function exactly like that.

Kyle was reminded of an arena as he wove through the stacks of aged leather cases, brand-new suits, and souvenirs from Taiwan, past ski boots and rain boots and a glass case full of watches. After a moment, he set out down an aisle of women's bathing suits. He imagined tired employees marking and cleaning an endless supply of swimwear. Another tropical vacation, they would say as they unzipped a flap, another pair of flip-flops. The concept somehow repulsed him. Ninety days didn't seem long enough to give up hope and sell someone's belongings. He walked past an elderly woman and examined a floral bikini. He imagined Bridget standing hopelessly by an empty conveyor belt, robbed of her own possessions. He imagined himself comforting her and assuring her they'd find it eventually. The girl who lost the floral bikini had probably thrown a fit, but Bridget would have been calm, forgiving, and it would have driven him crazy.

"There you are!" She came out from behind a rack of golf clubs. "I think I'm going to buy this shawl." Bridget pulled an antique-looking cloth around her shoulders and pointed her face up in a pose. "What do you think?"

"It's nice."

"Are you thinking of getting a new digital camera?" She folded the shawl back up and tucked her hair behind her ears. "Look, it's two for one."

"Maybe."

"Well, I'm going to go buy this before I change my mind," she said as she shifted her brown purse higher up on her shoulder and walked to the left, "but I'll come find you in a minute."

"Hey, Bridget." He didn't know what prompted him to say it. She stopped and turned around, her brown ponytail swinging to her left shoulder. Kyle opened his mouth, then shut it. "Uh, did you know that some guy once found an original Salvador Dalí print in here?"

"Yeah, I did," she said sharply, but he could see her roll her eyes and grin as she turned back toward the register.

Kyle looked up at the fluorescent lights and listened as their hum mixed with the distant music. She knows, he thought. She must have found it in the hotel. Kyle placed his backpack on a pile of black duffels and followed behind her. It wasn't until they were back in the parking lot that he decided to run inside and buy it back for $4.99.

Hail, Full of Grace

At the Unitarian Universalist Christmas pageant in Cambridge, Massachusetts, it didn't matter that Mary insisted on keeping her nails painted black or that Joseph had come out of the closet. On December 25th at seven and nine P.M., three Wise Women would follow the Wise Men down the aisle, one wearing a kimono and another African garb; instead of myrrh they would bring chicken soup, instead of frankincense they'd play lullabies. The shepherds had a line on protecting the environment and the innkeeper held a foreclosure sign. No one quite believed in God and no one quite didn't—so they made it about the songs and the candles and the pressing together of bodies on lacquered wooden pews.

My daughter Emma was the Jesus understudy. Five months into the adoption and the word still sounded strange.

"Your daughter's our backup baby?" the minister had asked.

"Emma is, yes." I shifted her upward in my arms. "She was just telling me how she hopes the leading Jesus sprains an ankle." He stared at me, but I thought it was funny.

* * *

I don't usually volunteer babies for debatably experimental Christmas pageants but Jared called me seven times the day before. There was a crisis. Jesus had to go to San Antonio to visit his grandmother in the hospital and the First Parish's annual nativity was famous for live babies. I was back in my hometown for Christmas and Jared, my best friend from high school, was the Community Outreach Chair and didn't want to talk about it. According to his phone, the church was only ten minutes from my house and Honestly, Audrey, do you really have an excuse? I didn't.

I was bored anyway. The newspaper had given me six months off and I was already craving deadlines. I'd come home a few weeks early before Christmas to spend time with my mother, who recommended the early arrival after she heard me describe the strangeness of having Emma alone in my apartment. The first month had been silent. I'd put music on sometimes but I was afraid of having the TV too loud. There was no fighting or laughing or lovemaking squeezed perfectly into the hours she fell asleep, and at my Monthly, Dr. Berenson recommended I talk to the baby. So I did. Just monologued while she was feeding or staring or falling asleep on my chest.

She was four months old, but I'd told her everything. Told her about my job and being bored with my book and the reason why I got her. Told her I was sorry I couldn't nurse her, sorry she had no father, sorry I kept talking to her all the time when she probably just wanted to sleep or eat or start mapping her world. One night, when she wouldn't stop crying, I told her about Julian. Told her how pathetic I was for still thinking that far back. I'm forty-two, I'd whispered while she gripped at a finger—you don't know this yet, but that's old to hold your hand.

I'd dated Julian from sixteen to twenty-three. We got together our sophomore year of high school and didn't break up until a year after our college graduations. Christmas meant coming home, and coming home meant Julian and I were thrust into the same eight-mile radius and forced to revisit the whole ordeal. I kept his holiday cards in a drawer in my apartment year after year: his three children aging and waving from beaches and backyards and trips to pick pumpkins.

* * *

On the evening of the twenty-fourth, I had Jared pick me up for the rehearsal. He was busy, but I didn't know how to get there and I wanted to talk to him. He didn't need convincing.

"You're saving my life, Audrey." He made a kissing noise into the phone. "I'll be there at four."

"Is Brett coming?" I caught him before he hung up.

"Why? Do you not want him to?"

"Either way."

"I'll leave him at the church."

"You're a doll, Jerry." I hung up before he would make the kissing noise again. It was a habit he'd picked up from Brett since they'd moved in together and it always made me hate him.

Emma pushed Cheerios off her high-chair tray when she heard his car crunch down the driveway of my old house. It was day five of cereal eating and Emma had already mastered the art of throwing. She stared at me once the cereal had successfully spilled off the edges and I imagined her throwing Cheerios out from inside the manger. It cracked me up, which cracked her up, and when she reached her arms into the air, I carried her upstairs with me to grab a red scarf for festivity. It was my mother's phrase, *for festivity.*

* * *

"Do I have to come?" I said when Jared opened the door.

"Nice to see you too." He plucked Emma out of my arms and cooed. "I'm taking baby Jesus regardless, so I'm guessing you're gonna want to get in the car." He walked straight in through the door like he had since he was ten.

"Tell me no one from high school is going to be there." The question hadn't occurred to me on the phone, but the prospect of parading Emma to my old friends as Jesus incarnate was horrifying. Jared didn't answer. "Is there any way to specify in the program that I didn't volunteer?"

"But you did volunteer!" he grinned, picking up the car seat and walking out to his Volvo. "I asked you and you said yes!"

Jared was the only one of us who'd never really left, but he understood that coming home was hard for me. Seven years is no small amount of time to date someone, no matter how young, and practically everything in our small town reminded me of Julian: our high school years when we went to proms and movies and our college summers when we passed the time smoking pot in his car, squealing to 7–Eleven with Jared and Lucas and Sarah and trading off sleeping in each other's twin-size beds. We were that couple. The one the single teachers envied at prom, the one everyone took for granted, for untouchable. Our senior year, we lost Cutest Couple to Skylar and Jillian, but it was only because Jillian's best friend was editor of the yearbook and Julian's soccer team voted against us as a joke. In the summer we traveled with each other's families and in the fall we ate at two Thanksgivings. He was nerdy but earnest, handsome but flirty. And I loved him.

I try to remember these months objectively but it's hard—and around thirty, they started to haunt me. His dimples and his collarbone and his compliments and the way my girlfriends' parents told my mother they were jealous. Sometimes I'd go months without thinking back, but the what-ifs always seemed to find me, creep up on me when I was lonely or tired or forced home for Christmas. He'd found someone else and I never did. Never even fell in love again. Not really.

* * *

Jared turned on the radio. All the stations were carols, so we just settled into it. "Winter Wonderland" played as we drove past salted pavement and snowless fields. The Charles was half frozen but the trees on Storrow Drive were still clutching their crinkled leaves.

"How are you doing?" Jared asked as we crossed the Eliot Bridge.

"Okay," I admitted. "I'm excited to get back to work but feel guilty for feeling that, if you know what I mean."

"Naw, that's normal," he said.

"How would you know?"

"Happened with all my babies." I shoved him and he smiled, then sobered. "But you've been okay, in New York?" I knew New York was a euphemism for "by yourself," but it was Jared and I didn't mind him asking.

"Yeah," I said, pausing to reach a hand back for Emma to squeeze. "I'm still struggling with . . . I'm still hoping that she . . . feels more like she's *mine*."

"Interesting."

"Not really," I said, feeling terrible for even articulating it. I pulled up my turtleneck and looked back out at the river. "To be honest, it's hard because she reminds me a lot of the other baby."

Jared was silent and kept his eyes on the road.

"It's been a long time, Audrey."

"I know," I said.

"She's okay. She's doing fine."

"I know she is. I know." I shifted my attention back into the car and sat up. "Look, you're the big bad Community Outreach Chair, we can just talk about it later."

"Okay," he said, shrugging his thin shoulders upward. I waited for him to protest, to insist that we discuss and overanalyze—but instead he started humming "Silent Night." "Wait till you see this pageant, Audrey, it's going to be insane. I have this girl playing Mary who we practically had to coax out of her goth clothing. A real sweetheart, don't get me wrong, and she's been practicing with the other Jesus all week so if we end up needing to swap in Emma, she'll be fine." He turned around to make a face at the baby and got a high-pitched squeal. And I realized he was right to change the subject.

* * *

I found out I was pregnant in December of my senior year at college. The night before, I'd told Julian I thought I'd gained weight at school. He didn't say anything, just looked at me with an expression of disgust. But when we went out to dinner the next night, neither of us touched the bread basket. Julian smiled at the waiter when he took it away, taking my hand and pinching at my knuckles.

We bought the test on our way home. It wasn't the first time. I was skinny then, missing my period a lot, and we always giggled in the car about what to buy along with it.

"I dare you to buy condoms," I'd say.

"I dare you to buy porn," he'd tease.

That night Julian chose to buy a bag of Skittles and we shared his peace offering while we waited until I had to pee.

When the test came back positive, we drove back to CVS and bought three more. We made the mistake of telling our parents and everyone seemed to have opinions. The Elks were Catholic and that was pretty much it. Julian wanted to keep it. He told me it wouldn't matter—that *I* was what mattered. That he'd love me. That we could get married.

My mother disagreed. My dad was Jewish and my mom was nothing, and to them, pregnancy was a choice.

I was somewhere in between.

"You don't understand," I told her that night. "You *wish* Dad looked at you the way Julian looks at me." She stopped sorting clothes and let the quiet settle.

"I know," she said. "If you loved him less, I'd tell you to have it."

I told her she didn't make sense. I told her there were options. I told her she was just jealous and heartless and it was my body and he wanted it and I loved him so I *had* to have it. I had to. She didn't understand. She was aged and stubborn and she didn't understand.

That Sunday, Julian and I went for a walk along the reservoir.

"We don't have to keep it," he said. "But if you love me, please, don't kill it."

So I had it. For him. And we gave our six pounds, fourteen ounces to a couple from New Hampshire on August 19, 1989. They came to pick her up two days after I'd gone into labor. They did it in another room; the literature said it was best not to meet adoptive parents. Julian wanted it open, but I wanted it closed. So we signed our names on dotted lines that even eighteen years wouldn't undo. *No, I do not want my birth child contacting me. No, I do not want the progress reports.*

* * *

The Unitarian Universalist church in Cambridge, Massachusetts, was stone and beautiful and surrounded by bumper-stickered cars. It was cold out, and I was worried about Emma, so I pressed her tiny face to my neck as we dashed from Jared's sedan to the basement's back door. The place was packed with screaming children dressed like animals and bearded shepherds herding angels upstairs. The basement smelled like attic and the costumes were dated but the energy circling the room was powerful and warm. A rainbow flag hung next to a bulletin board and painted Plato quotes wrapped the room's upper wall. A girl with a head scarf was buried in her cell phone and Joseph appeared to be flirting with a Wise Man. The moment we entered, Emma started wailing, and the entire tableau seemed to freeze and face us. A gray-haired man in the middle smiled at me and I knew he was the minister even before I saw his robes. He didn't say anything but held his hands out slightly to his sides, palms out and fingers spread. I nodded back and shifted Emma around so everyone could see.

The pageant director was a chubby man in his fifties. He cupped my elbow in his palm while he explained the procedures and walked through the logistics for the following day. I was to sit in the front row and hold Emma wrapped in blue cloth in my lap. Henry, the Stouffers' baby, was the first baby Jesus; however, should he start crying or moving around, the director would give me the sign, Ms. Stouffer would take Henry down to the basement, and I would move forward and hand Emma to Mary. Conceptually, it seemed a bit bizarre. But I was assured elbow-in-hand that two babies were essential, so I smiled at him with only my eyes and pretended my head hurt so I could go back downstairs.

I saw my first pageant in Mesnil-le-Roi, just outside Paris, when I was in France the year after graduation. There was a Swiss boy and it was his idea, but it was stuffy and the goats smelled so we left and went back to his apartment. I'd thought I'd have a different mind in France—but when I landed at de Gaulle, it was still me. I worked in a school and walked around on weekends trying to force bohemia. When I came home, I was yearning for someone to whisper to, but everyone was twenty-three and living in New York.

Julian and I broke up just before I left. We'd tried to make it work after the adoption, but things were never quite the same. Giving her away was my decision and, like it or not, Julian understood what it meant. The baby asked if we really meant our forevers; he said yes, and I said I didn't know. I wanted to experience the world and meet new people and everyone says you're supposed to be single for at least some time. He tried to get me back, but not for too long.

The problem was, I'd broken up with him while I was still in love, so I never had the time to let it wash out. My mom said I shouldn't marry the first guy I dated and my friend Eliza had said I looked like I was bored. But I never met anyone better. I dated other men, but I seemed to pass them by, waiting for someone who'd trace my back while I slept and take me to church on Sundays. I'd meet *Him* in Paris, after Paris, in graduate school, at work. But each location passed as I rolled them off my shoulders. My sister called it a fluke at Thanksgiving one year when a friend of our aunt's asked about my husband.

"It's strange," she'd said, passing the gravy. And I'd felt a sudden urge to pour it on her head.

* * *

When I got back home that night, everyone was in the kitchen and living room preparing for dinner. My sister, her husband Alex, their sons Michael and Gabriel, my brother Henry, his wife Zoe, and their three children, Annabel, David, and Toby. My mother was thrilled to have her family reassembled and she scrambled around the kitchen, assigning tasks and things to chop. When I opened the door, everyone ran over to hold Emma and I could see my mother smiling behind the island in the center of the kitchen. The adoption was far less of an event than the births of my nieces and nephews and I specifically requested that I didn't want a shower or any public announcement. My sister had driven up in October, but it was the first time Henry or any of the kids had met Emma.

"Meet your new cousin," he said to Annabel, who was thirteen and held her arms out immediately.

"Oh my God," she cooed. "She's adorable. I love her!"

"Annabel was just saying in the car how excited she was to meet Emma," Zoe explained. "She doesn't have a sister so she was saying she wanted to give Emma all her old dolls when she's older."

"Wow," I said, wide-eyed. "Annabel, that's so kind of you. How grown-up."

I tried to imagine what Emma might look like when she was thirteen but I only saw another version of Annabel. Inevitably, I'd thought of this same scene a hundred times when I was younger: Julian's and my child meeting her new family in some kitchen somewhere. She was probably in that same kitchen right now—eating Christmas dinner, if her family even celebrated the holiday.

Still, it was nice to get attention for once, and not have to give it. The prospect of bringing Emma to every family holiday from now on filled me with a kind of comfort, and the idea of her older cousins playing with her and teasing her made me extremely glad. I tried to forget my (rarely expressed) concerns that the whole thing was a big mistake, and for the most part I managed. Seeing her inside my family gave it all a little context, and I was proud to be bouncing her on my knee while the adults sipped decaf coffees at the end of the night.

Christmas Day was the same as it always was—only I'd woken up early with my brother and sister to make a little stocking for Emma that I unpacked later while Henry held her up so she could watch. Zoe had planned to cook French-bread French toast with a fresh strawberry sauce but she'd forgotten to get enough eggs, so I volunteered to make a quick trip to Whole Foods, the only market nearby that'd be open. I tried to take Emma with me but my mother insisted I leave her.

"It's fine," she'd said. "I had a few of these myself." I looked at Emma, clutching a new stuffed snowman, and watched her blink at me, gnawing. I wondered for a moment how well she could recognize me but dismissed the thought as ridiculous. Emma didn't cry too often with the particular request of being returned to my arms and it sometimes made me insecure.

* * *

I ran into him at the supermarket. Of course. The last time it'd happened was three years ago at the liquor store on Christmas Eve. I saw him before he saw me, holding a slip of paper and roaming down the spice aisle. He looked good, the same, slightly pudgier than he was a few years ago, but still sporting his mop of curly brown hair. My reaction to his presence was always visceral, and I felt my hands start to shake slightly as I watched him. It struck me in that instant that I could have just turned around, walked to another aisle, and avoided the encounter. But I didn't even consider it.

"Jules," I said. The nickname came out by accident. He turned around, looked at me, and we both stared, then grinned.

"Of course," he said.

"I know."

"Just—of course," he said.

"I know."

We hugged and it was only slightly awkward. We communicated occasionally via e-mail, but I hadn't told him about Emma yet.

"How are you?"

"Good, good. How are you?"

"Good."

"Glad we got all those details out of the way," he said, smiling.

"I uh . . . I saw your Christmas card. Your oldest is getting . . . big." I was looking down, suddenly. Desperate for the conversation to flow smoothly.

"Yeah," Julian said. "He's nearly fifteen." He was studying me. We stood there for a few more seconds, just taking each other in.

"How's, uh . . ." I could tell he didn't know what to ask. ". . . the newspaper. Are you still . . . ?"

I interrupted him. "I'm taking some time off."

"To work on the book?"

"No, actually, to raise my daughter." I hardly used that word and it felt strange to say aloud. He looked at me and his mouth hinged open.

"Oh! Oh my gosh. Wow, Audrey, congratulations!"

"Thank you."

"Who's the, um, did you . . ." I saw his eyes dart to my left hand and back again.

"Adoption," I said. Nodding with my mouth closed and then trying a small smile, waving my hands at my sides. "The irony!" But he didn't laugh, and I could tell it still hurt him like it hurt me. We stood in silence again, rocking.

"What are you looking for?" The subject change was pathetic.

"Coriander," he said. "Apparently it's essential, so I offered to run out. You?"

"Eggs."

"Ah." Silence again. Then he smiled. "Is her name Emma?"

I nodded.

"You never got your Chloe, did you?" I said.

"I didn't," he laughed. "Alexis didn't like it." The thought of his wife made me uneasy and I realized, suddenly, that I should say I had to go.

"Listen." I took a step toward him. "I need to run home, but if you want to meet her, stop by the First Parish service tonight when you leave St. Andrew's. Nine o'clock. Jared roped me into having her play Jesus. Well, understudy for Jesus."

"You're kidding," he said. "I miss Jared. He's ridiculous."

"Everyone does."

"Well, I'll be there." He shifted his bag up on his shoulder. "Nine o'clock First Parish?"

"Nine o'clock First Parish."

* * *

I convinced my family, finally, that they didn't have to come "be supportive," and I drove Emma alone to the church and held her in the basement amid the sea of swarming children, parents, costumes, and cardboard. Jared arrived a little after I did and led me to my seat in the front pew slightly before the pageant was scheduled to start.

"Hi," he said, kissing me on the cheek.

"Hi," I said. "Merry Christmas."

"Merry Christmas." I waited for a second but then went on with it.

"I ran into Julian at the supermarket today."

"Of course you did."

"I know."

"Was it . . . ?"

I cut him off. "It was fine."

"Did you . . . ?"

"Yeah." I took a moment. "He knew her name was Emma." I decided to leave out the part about inviting him, but I scanned the crowd obsessively as the congregation built like a wave behind me. I was undercover—smuggling a baby Jesus whom no one else could see. I imagined *The Tempest*, the mythologies, and all the secret sets of twins I'd spent so long assessing in grad school. But then they lit the candles, so I stopped imagining and searching and tried to think about the present.

It was pitiable, pathetic, but I wanted him to come. Wanted him there, badly, to see me and Emma and understand that this was hard but that I wanted it. That it was hard but I was *okay*. But the pews were nearly filled and I didn't see him.

They dimmed the lights and I held Emma tight in my arms. I looked behind me and saw an old man writing in a notebook. Behind him, a kid yanking at his mother's shirt. To their left, shadowed by the balcony, a young couple pressing together and sharing a program. The boy was lanky and freckled and the girl was petite. She traced tiny circles into his palm, toying with his hand on her lap. The girl whispered something in his ear and he shook his head. She offered him a piece of gum and he refused. I looked away as the backlights faded, but I could just make out the boy pulling his hand away. I remembered a party in the city I hadn't thought of in years when I'd told Julian not to hold my hand because it was juvenile. I remembered wanting both hands that night—for gestures and hugs and brushing back my hair. That's the feeling I needed to remember, I thought. Not those nights in his car.

* * *

A small boy walked down the aisle with a giant North Star and the choir began a version of "The First Noel." I breathed in the pastor and the warmth of the other bodies. The wise men came and the shepherds and the sheep. I looked behind me again but I still didn't see Julian. The candles on the chalice dripped wax onto the lambs and the songs from the choir made the angels start flying. More angels came, and the kings and the queens. I looked back again but the door was still shut. He wasn't coming.

Somewhere, buried in the manger, a baby was crying. It screamed and shrieked to the decrescendo of "Silent Night." Somewhere, someone was making a sign; somewhere, Jared was gesturing furiously. The Wise Men shrugged and Mary started crying. But I didn't notice. Emma had her tiny hand wrapped around my finger. I pressed her against me until the song had ended. Until the dust started falling like snow and I could feel her tiny breath on my neck. My daughter, I thought, was not twenty-two and home from some college with a family I didn't know. She was breathing against my chest as the pews sank and rose.

I heard the creak of a door behind me and turned, quickly, to see Julian shutting its heavy frame behind him, panting. Jared's hands were on Emma and I felt him pulling and myself letting go.

Sclerotherapy

Karen found out the tattoo of the Chinese character on her right ankle actually meant *soybean* five months after she got it. *Inner resolve and outer peace, a general levelheadedness and tranquility* was the translation printed under the thin black character she had chosen from the chart on the wall. *Soybean* was the translation her brother's Asian roommate awkwardly gave her after she modeled it for him in the smoky dorm room on the fifth floor. He asked if the artist was Chinese, and she shook her head. She asked if he was high, and he shook his. Karen slid the leg of her jeans back down and bit at a nail. The roommate fidgeted. *I mean, he probably just copied them onto the chart from a takeout menu.* The tang of incense clung to Karen as she walked down five flights of stairs.

* * *

"So it's five veins today, right?" The nurse made small movements with her pencil as she flipped between thin papers on a clipboard. Karen didn't respond but shifted her weight back in the chair. The thickly set woman pushed her lips out and adjusted the waistband of her brightly patterned scrubs. "Five veins, yes?" The question was repeated slowly, with an emphasis on the word *five*.

"That's what they tell me." She was a woman of sixty-two; it wasn't her first time sitting in the polyester recliner. Wasn't the first time the thick substance would be injected carefully into her calves. She hated the experience. Not just the pain of her legs thickening then thinning, but also the two-hour view of nothing but her ankles. Socks were usually the solution, folded down and over the youthful rebelliousness stamped above her anklebone. But in the Sclerotherapy Clinic, there were no ridged socks to cover her shins, and no smile to cover her keen self-consciousness. In the Sclerotherapy Clinic, she thought, there were only fat nurses and varicose veins.

The blood in Karen's veins was beginning to drain out. Her body lay inflexibly strapped to the recliner, tilted at a harsh angle so her feet were raised high above her head. The sting of the injected gel still tingled over her skin, making the thin unshaven hairs on her legs stand up.

"All right now, Karen, try to relax." The nurse opened a small drawer and removed a bundle of compression stockings. "I'm sure you know the drill by now." She squirted down the nozzle of a Lubriderm bottle and thick white lotion plopped into her hand. "But remember, you can't take these things off for two weeks unless you're lying down." Her hands rubbed each other and attained an oily glisten in the office light. "Your veins gotta glue themselves together, see, so the blood is forced to find another path." Karen nodded and blinked slowly.

* * *

What does it mean? she had been asked by a coworker one spring about twenty years ago when sweat had rubbed the usual Band-Aid off her ankle. Karen tugged at her earlobe. *It means inner resolve and outer peace, a general levelheadedness and tranquil-*

ity. The woman nodded, smiled politely, and turned back to her desk. I was nineteen, Karen said, almost sarcastically. She opened her mouth again but realized she had nothing to say. The question always bothered her. Made her hate herself more with each false explanation. But she kept at it, as if it might somehow compensate for having *soybean* etched permanently into her skin. Karen swung her chair left and stared into her computer screen. The case she was studying stared back, its importance suddenly mocking her.

* * *

"Oh." The nurse paused. "I didn't know you had a tattoo, miss." She grinned slightly. "What does it mean?" Karen had expected it. In fact, she was surprised it had taken this long.

"It means inner resolve and outer peace, a general level-headedness and tranquility." She lied, she thought, for the same reason she was getting her varicose veins removed. The nurse exhaled and tucked her hair behind her ears.

"That's nice. Very peaceful." She began unbuckling Karen's legs. "Did you get it in China?"

"No. I got it in Brooklyn. I was nineteen." The nurse carefully lifted her calves and started pulling the beige compression stockings over her skin.

* * *

The edamame jeered at her. She was trying to enjoy herself, but this type of thing always seemed to happen at Chinese restaurants. If it hadn't been her daughter's choice, if she hadn't just returned from college and if they hadn't been meeting her really-serious-this-time boyfriend, she would have objected. But it was all of those things, so she kept her mouth shut.

So, Brian—Karen looked up at him—*I hear you're thinking*

about business school. Brian responded, but the answer sort of floated through her. She imagined the black lines on her ankle thickening with glee as she slowly filled her body with soybeans. Karen wondered if she was as pathetic as this thought suggested. If she was so preoccupied with her own sense of herself that basic conversation was beyond her. She looked up at Brian and nodded. *I see.* His hand was resting on her daughter's next to the chopsticks.

It had been months, maybe years, since she had actually thought about it. It wasn't something that entered her daily musings. Socks on during the day, socks off at night; dresses and skirts meant Band-Aids: an almost unconscious ritual in her routine. Karen glanced at the couple glancing at each other. She wondered if Brian could be put in the category of impulsive decisions. If he was her daughter's version of not bothering to consult a language dictionary.

* * *

"There you are, all done." The compression stockings were tight around her thighs now and the polyester recliner was humming as it tilted slowly upward. The room seemed slightly darker than when she had entered, and the lack of light peering through the edges of the blinds told her it was probably late afternoon. The nurse walked to the corner and began rinsing her hands.

Karen studied her legs. Her varicose veins no longer popped out like tributaries leading to her ankle, but she wasn't pleased. The thin dark outlines could still be seen slightly beneath the lean nylon of the stockings. Images of her brother's incense-hazed dorm, the coworker at her firm, and the evening when she first met her son-in-law drifted in her head. She gently placed her feet on the floor and lifted her weight down off the chair. Some things, Karen thought, couldn't be flattened at the Sclerotherapy Clinic.

"Take care now, ma'am." The nurse was drying her hands on a paper towel.

"My tattoo," Karen said, pausing in the doorway before shutting it behind her, "actually means soybean."

Challenger Deep

When the jellyfish came, we woke everyone up. They floated down on the ship like snow and even Lev came into the sail to press his face on the periscope. The glow was dim but we could see our arms and outlines and after a minute we stepped away from the glass to look at each other's eyes. No one said anything, not even the Captain, and I could hear Ellen breathing hard against the glass. My eyes hurt from seeing but there was a strange hope in the blue light, and the weeks of darkness drew us toward it like moths. The five of us sat on the steel for what must have been an hour before the fluorescent specks drifted out and the submarine returned to its blackness. Eventually, I heard the Captain stand up—but it was a while before he finally cleared his throat and felt his way back to the controls.

We couldn't see anything. Not even our fingers flexing in front of our faces or the steel walls we ran our hands along as we passed through chambers. We were thirty-six thousand feet under when the ballast tanks broke and the pressure gauge short-circuited the electrics. The power was on but the lights couldn't be fixed from inside. I wasn't angry like the others. Lev would pace around and scream things in Russian or slam his fist against a door, but he was young and louder than the rest of us. I preferred the days when no one spoke, or at least not about the surface. There wasn't a point, I told them once while we were eating dehydrateds, there's really no point.

I waited by the periscope for the rest of C shift because it was my sleep break anyway and I wanted to see if the currents changed and the jellyfish came back. I sat there for a while but they never came so I pulled out the ripped piece of shirt to tie back around my eyes. It's easier when you pretend to be blindfolded. I heard this on a cave tour in Arizona but Ellen was the only other crew member who listened. It was a small ship, only an Alvin II, so I could pass whomever I wanted to if I took the right turns. I heard Lev talking to the Captain by the desalination tank, which was easy to find because of its dull hum.

"We'd know if we were rising." The Captain must have been sitting down.

"Maybe not, sir. Maybe the pressure streams are different in the trench."

"We'd know," he repeated. "We'd feel it."

"Then how do you explain the goddamn fluorescence? You know damn well cnidarians can't survive in near freezing!" He was pacing now.

"The geysers are heated—"

"The geysers are heated. *Poshol na khui, suka!*" He kicked the metal and I inhaled.

"Ellen?" The Captain had heard me. I was always accidentally listening in because I couldn't think of anything to say.

"No, sir. It's Patrick," I said. "I was just coming back from the sail. Wanted to make sure we didn't miss them if they came back."

"They're not coming back." It was Lev's voice and I heard him lean against the wall. I waited for the Captain to reply but he didn't.

"I just wanted to make sure." There was silence and I could hear Hyun clicking the switchboard down the passage. He was Korean and couldn't really speak English but he was the best technician at Woods Hole lab. We listened to his taps for a while until we fell back into ourselves. The Captain walked over to the air vent so it blew on his face and hair. I knew everyone was zooming out, imagining once again what we looked like from far away.

"It was nice," Lev finally said from the wall. "I forgot what it was like."

"I know," the Captain said. "My hands."

I pictured the tiny dots floating out like stars. The way it looked like outer space from the periscope windows. For the first time in a long time I thought about my sister and the house I lived in as a child. Lev stood up and walked out to his berth. He didn't leave at B shift but there wasn't much we could do about allocations anymore.

* * *

We had no concept of time and soon the darkness made it hard to remember what was real. I'd imagine tables that weren't there and reach for railings that had never existed. After a while I stopped having visual dreams, shifting in my sheets as my mind recounted sounds and sensations that were all cold or steel or underwater. We talked less about trees and more about nothing, playing endless games to name the elements or species of fish until one of us would hit something or start crying or simply not respond.

Once when we were all together, Lev wondered aloud whether China had a deep-capacity submarine that no one knew about. It was stupid, but we spent the next three days hypothesizing about why and how the international community might be able to procure it and send it down to get us out. Ellen believed it most of all because she was in love with a man named Daniel who lived in London. She told me when we were cleaning the interhull vents and the other three were sleeping. I'm not sure why she decided to tell me—probably because I don't say much. She was skinny for thirty and wore a blindfold like me. I remembered then that she'd told us this was her first real dive.

"He's a teacher," she said softly. "We met online through this website." I'd heard that this could happen but I didn't really understand how. I took the solution and ran it on a cloth pipe through the holes. When she sat up, her braid flew up and fell again on her back with a small thud. "We haven't made real plans but I think we're going to get married." Ellen was the only one who still spoke about home in the present tense.

"What does he teach?" I wasn't sure what to ask.

"Social studies." She paused. "I did my marine PhD at Cambridge so that's why we met." I was trying to get the dust from the vent sheets but I couldn't see whether or not it was working. Ellen was working too and I liked that about her. She wasn't a very pretty girl if my memory was right, but she had really long hair and her eyes were a sort of green. "I don't—" But she broke off.

We worked for a while until it was mostly done and then I asked if she wanted to eat now or later and she said now. We traced our way to the dry box that held our rations and added water to the powdery protein mix. Regulations required six months of meals on all H-certified vessels, and the Alvin II was about eight weeks into what should have been a two-week Experimental. We sat at the small half-counter and ate until Ellen fell quiet and started to shake. For the first time in my life I think I was happy to be alone. I wouldn't want anyone up there to be shaking for me.

* * *

It wasn't long before people started whispering. The darkness and circles were getting unbearable and most of us were beginning to crack in our own ways. Lev started advocating for "alternatives" to waiting it out. There wasn't enough food. No sub could go deep enough. It was now or six months from now. But the ship required five people to operate it, so everyone had to agree before anything was going to happen. I disagreed at first but the idea had fallen like a seed. I felt it when I lay in my berth, when I tried to sleep, when I had dark dreams, and when I half-woke to eat protein and walk around the same five rooms in the same five patterns until I slept and had the same dark dreams.

Ellen didn't want to. No one needed to ask anyone else because it was just obvious. Hyun and the Captain were too rational not to agree, and Lev was the first one to really lose it. He started groaning and hitting his head from inside his door. The Captain admitted that he could still see in his dreams. He rushed through his maintenance so he could close and open his eyes. If the lights hadn't gone when the pressure snapped the ballast tanks I think things might have been different. I think we might have been able to wait until the powder ran out.

"Here!" Lev screamed from the center control. "Here, here, now!" He was shrieking and we could hear banging so we all ran to the control. The Captain sat Lev down until he stopped thrashing. Hyun seemed scared and Ellen was hanging back to the side.

"I can't do it," said Lev. We couldn't see him but we could hear the violent quiver in his voice. "I'm sorry. Look, I can't do it. I see things in my head. Faces and all the water, it's . . . *My zdes' umryom. Vy vse ponimaete, chto my budem zhdat' i zhdat', i potom mu vse umryom.* There are voices and—the darkness and—" He erupted into a sob and the Captain went over and must have put his hands on his shoulders because he quieted down. Hyun never said much but we heard his quiet voice speak up from Lev's other side.

"Yes," he said. "Yes. No more do." I didn't say anything and neither did the Captain but everyone understood that we couldn't. We needed to wait. We heard Ellen inhale like she might say something but her lips closed and she shifted her feet. There was a silence and I almost said something about the time or temperature gauges but then Ellen finally spoke.

"I just . . ." She paused. "I just . . . there's no point in not waiting. They might . . . it's not impossible."

"It's impossible." Lev spoke the words quietly, straightfor-wardly. She was hurt. "It's impossible," Lev repeated, louder. But Ellen had shifted to move and walked out of the room. I heard the Captain run his hands through his hair.

"She has someone," I said. "We have to wait for her. We have to wait for her because he's in England and Ellen . . ." No one said anything and we waited in that room for a long time until Lev began rocking in his seat again. I started thinking about trees even though I knew it would only make the ach-ing worse.

* * *

Things were different after that. We became suspicious of each other, of all two-person conversations. Ellen didn't talk to anyone much, but we knew she was listening. I passed her one night standing by the dry box. I wasn't sure what she was doing with it open but I wondered if maybe she was trying to calculate portions or time. There were five shift jobs and five people so we couldn't run the ship without all of us. Lev might have been crazy, but he knew this too and he knew we all had to agree. So we waited. We waited two weeks until one day after circuit repairs when I couldn't hear Ellen in her station.

I thought she might be upset in her berth so I walked by her door. I wanted to tell her that it was okay and that we were going to wait, that there was no rush. We could make it half a year if we wanted to. We could wait. But she wasn't in there. She wasn't by the dry box or desalinator and when I screamed her name it rang through the steel of the ship but there was no response. Then I heard Hyun's tiny voice call back from a passage that we hadn't used since before it got dark.

The Captain came running and we fumbled for the switch that pushed the door to the launching suits. When it was open, we couldn't see but I started brushing my arms as fast as I could along the floor where the wires were stored, feeling one, two, three, and then it was missing. There were only four deep-water suits and I think we all realized at once what had happened. We opened the screen vent to the anteroom that opened out to the water and pulled in the cord with the autosimulator. The ocean was black just like the walls so when we heard her body thump into the chamber we couldn't tell. I ran in and felt the cold on her face and the wet on the suit, but the veins in her neck were still throbbing. She'd cracked the helmet, and her face had ice shards on the sides.

"Ellen!" I screamed, but she didn't respond. "Ellen! Ellen!" Then I realized what had happened. What the depth had done. I shook her quickly, and she stirred, coughed, choked over to the side. I moved immediately to her ears and felt the warm blood trickling out and into her long black hair. Her eardrums had burst and she was trapped in darkness and silence and a giant iron suit. We moved it off her and her hand reached up to touch my face. It felt strange and I wanted to move away but I let her feel my nose and mouth and eyes until she knew it was me. She'd done it on purpose but she didn't know we'd find her in time.

"She's deaf," the Captain said. Lev was groaning again from the other room. We didn't know what to do so we carried her into the counter room, heated water, and poured it on her over her clothes. It felt darker than it used to, and I wondered for a minute if that was possible. If we had drifted into a trench of the trench where we would soon hear tectonics crunch into lava and draw us down.

Ellen moaned. I ripped my blindfold cloth in two and balled it up into her ears to stop the bleeding. She lay there like that for a long time until she was quiet. We gave her food and she seemed like she was okay so we moved her into her berth and went back to our stations. I could hear Lev pacing and Hyun clicking and the comfort of the desalinator hum and ventilator air and imagined Ellen alone in the silence of her world—confined entirely to the universe of her thoughts and half-drawn memories of days somewhere in England.

She emerged much later with her arms outstretched, feeling around corners she already knew by heart. We'd squeeze her shoulder when we passed, but that was all we knew how to do. She was lost. And the reality of her attempt had silenced our philosophizing. We were waiting now. We ate and moved and ate and moved.

* * *

I was on Sonar Detect when we picked up the signal from the rover. It had no metal detection and looked like it'd been traveling blind straight through the trench. It was small, robotic, and probably the only thing they could construct to withhold the pressure in limited time. Lev went running and screamed and I guess Ellen could feel the vibrations he made on the floor because I heard her door shut behind her.

"It's audio," said the Captain. "There's an antenna. No one's coming." We turned up the sonar controls and heard a short five-minute clip play twice through the wave detectors before it slipped past in its motion and out of sight. They knew our range and they knew we'd have five minutes to hear it on either side. It was expensive, I could tell by the frequency. A million-dollar message.

It was my sister and the Captain's old lieutenant and Lev's best friend and Hyun's mom. The last voice was Daniel's and it spoke in a shaky whisper: "Ellen, I love you. Ellen, I can't look at the ocean anymore." He went on but I was too dazed to remember more. Ellen moaned and walked around, confused. Daniel, I traced on her arm. Slowly, so she could comprehend each letter. A message. She didn't understand. My hand was shaking, so I did it slower. A message. The ocean. He loves you. But we couldn't remember any more—our own thoughts scratched with our own words. She jerked away and went wandering back through the ship until we found her later, collapsed and sleeping by the vent.

* * *

The hours blurred as our food box emptied, but I never stopped dreaming black dreams. Sometimes, when the Captain was at the controls or Lev was asleep, I'd climb into the sail and stare through the periscope at the thousands of leagues. I closed my eyes and saw stars but the jellyfish never came.

NONFICTION

So what I'm trying to say is you should text me back.
Because there's a precedent. Because there's an urgency.
Because there's a bedtime.
Because when the world ends I might not have my phone
   charged and
If you don't respond soon,
I won't know if you'd wanna leave your shadow next to mine.

—*Marina Keegan, from the poem "Nuclear Spring"*

Stability in Motion

My 1990 Camry's DNA was designed inside the metallic walls of the Toyota Multinational Corporation's headquarters in Tokyo, Japan; transported via blueprint to the North American Manufacturing nerve center in Hebron, Kentucky; grown organ by organ in four major assembly plants in Alabama, New Jersey, Texas, and New York; trucked to 149 Arsenal Street in Watertown, Massachusetts; and steered home by my grandmother on September 4, 1990. It featured a 200 hp, 3.0 L V6 engine, a four-speed automatic, and an adaptive Variable Suspension System. She deemed the car too "high tech." In 1990 this meant a cassette player, a cup holder, and a manually operated moon roof.

During its youth, the car traveled little. In fifteen years my grandmother accumulated a meager twenty-five thousand miles, mostly to and from the market, my family's house, and the Greek jewelry store downtown. The black exterior remained glossy and spotless, the beige interior crisp and pristine. Tissues were disposed of, seats vacuumed, and food prohibited. My grandmother's old-fashioned cleanliness was an endearing virtue—one that I evidently did not inherit.

I acquired the old Camry through an awkward transaction. Ten days before my sixteenth birthday, my grandfather died.

He was eighty-six and it had been long expected, yet I still felt a guilty unease when I heard the now surplus car would soon belong to me. For my grandmother, it was a symbolic good-bye. She needed to see only *one* car in her garage—needed to comprehend her loss more tangibly. Grandpa's car was the "nicer" of the two, so that one she would keep. Three weeks after the funeral, my grandmother and I went to the bank, I signed a check for exactly one dollar, and the car was legally mine. That was that. When I drove her home that evening, I manually opened the moon roof and put on a tape of Frank Sinatra. My grandma smiled for the first time in weeks.

Throughout the next three years, the car evolved. When I first parked the Toyota in my driveway, it was spotless, full of gas, and equipped with my grandmother's version of survival necessities. The glove compartment had a magnifying glass, three pens, and the registration in a little Ziploc bag. The trunk had two matching black umbrellas, a first aid kit, and a miniature sewing box for emergency repairs. Like my grandmother's wrists, everything smelled of Opium perfume.

For a while, I maintained this immaculate condition. Yet one Wrigley's wrapper led to two and soon enough my car underwent a radical transformation—the vehicular equivalent of a midlife crisis. Born and raised in proper formality, the car saw me as *that* friend from school, the bad example who washes away naïveté and corrupts the clean and innocent. We were the same age, after all—both eighteen. The Toyota was born again, crammed with clutter, and exposed to decibel levels it had never fathomed. I filled it with giggling friends and emotional phone calls, borrowed skirts and bottled drinks.

The messiness crept up on me. Parts of my life began falling off, forming an eclectic debris that dribbled gradually into every corner. Empty sushi containers, Diet Coke cans, half-full packs of gum, sweaters, sweatshirts, socks, my running shoes. My clutter was nondiscriminatory. I had every variety of newspaper, scratched-up English paper, biology review sheet, and Spanish flash card discarded on the seats after I'd sufficiently studied on my way to school. The left door pocket was filled with tiny tinfoil balls, crumpled after consuming my morning English muffin. By Friday, I had the entire house's supply of portable coffee mugs. By Sunday, someone always complained about their absence and I would rush out, grab them all, and surreptitiously place them in the dishwasher.

My car was not gross; it was occupied, cluttered, cramped. It became an extension of my bedroom, and thus an extension of myself. I had two bumper stickers on the back: REPUBLICANS FOR VOLDEMORT and the symbol for the Equal Rights Campaign. On the back side windows were OBAMA '08 signs that my parents made me take down because they "dangerously blocked my sight lines." The trunk housed my guitar but was also the library, filled with textbooks and novels, the giant tattered copy of *The Complete Works of William Shakespeare* and all one hundred chapters of *Harry Potter* on tape. A few stray cassettes littered the corners, their little brown insides ripped out, tangled and mutilated. They were the casualties of the trunk trenches, sprawled out forgotten next to the headband I never gave back to Meghan.

On average, I spent two hours a day driving. It was nearly an hour each way to school, and the old-fashioned Toyota—regarded with lighthearted amusement by my classmates—came to be a place of comfort and solitude amid the chaos of my daily routine. My mind was free to wander, my muscles to relax. No one was watching or keeping score. Sometimes I let the deep baritone of NPR's Tom Ashbrook lecture me on oil shortages. Other times I played repetitive mix tapes with titles like *Pancake Breakfast, Tie-Dye and Granola,* and *Songs for the Highway When It's Snowing.*

Ravaging my car, I often found more than just physical relics. For two months I could hardly open the side door without reliving the first time he kissed me. His dimpled smile was barely visible in the darkness, but it nevertheless made me stumble backward when I found my way blushingly back into the car. On the backseat there was the June 3 issue of the *New York Times* that I couldn't bear to throw out. When we drove home together from the camping trip, he read it cover to cover while I played Simon and Garfunkel—hoping he'd realize all the songs were about us. We didn't talk much during that ride. We didn't need to. He slid his hand into mine for the first time when we got off the highway; it was only after I made my exit that I realized I should have missed it. Above this newspaper are the fingernail marks I dug into the leather of my steering wheel on the night we decided to *just be friends.* My car listened to me cry for all twenty-two-and-a-half miles home.

The physical manifestations of my memories soon crowded the car. My right back speaker was broken from the time my older brother and I pulled an all-nighter singing shamelessly during our rainy drive home from the wedding. I remember the sheer energy of the storm, the lights, the music—moving through us, transcending the car's steel shell, and tracing the city. There was the folder left behind from the day I drove my dad to an interview the month after he lost his job. It was coincidental that *his* car was in the shop, but I knew he felt more pathetic that it was he, not his daughter, in the passenger seat. I kept my eyes on the road, feeling the confused sadness of a child who catches a parent crying.

I talked a lot in my car. Thousands of words and songs and swears are absorbed in its fabric, just like the orange juice I spilled on my way to the dentist. It knows what happened when Allie went to Puerto Rico, understands the difference between the way I look at Nick and the way I look at Adam, and remembers the first time I experimented with talking to myself. I've practiced for auditions, college interviews, Spanish oral presentations, and debates. There's something novel about swearing alone in the car. Yet with the pressures of APs and SATs and the other acronyms that haunt high school, the act became more frequent and less refreshing.

My car has seen three drive-in movies. During *The Dark Knight*, its battery died and, giggling ferociously, we had to ask the overweight family in the next row to jump it. The smell of popcorn permeated every crevice of the sedan, and all rides for the next week were like a trip to the movies. There was a variety of smells in the Camry. At first it smelled like my grandmother—perfume, mint, and mothballs. I went through a chai-tea phase during which my car smelled incessantly of Indian herbs. Some mornings it would smell slightly of tobacco and I would know immediately that my older brother had kidnapped it the night before. For exactly three days it reeked of marijuana. Dan had removed the shabbily rolled joint from behind his ear and our fingers had trembled as the five of us apprehensively inhaled. Nothing happened. Only the seats seemed to absorb the plant and get high. Mostly, however, it smelled like nothing to me. Yet when I drove my friends, they always said it had a distinct aroma. I believe this functioned in the same way as not being able to taste your own saliva or smell your own odor—the car and I were pleasantly immune to each other.

In the Buckingham Browne & Nichols High School year-book I was voted worst driver, but on most days I will refute this superlative. My car's love for parking tickets made me an easy target, but I rarely received other violations. My mistakes mostly harmed me, not others—locking my keys in the car or parking on the wrong side of the road. Once, last winter, I needed to refill my windshield wiper fluid and in a rushed frenzy poured an entire bottle of similarly blue antifreeze inside. Antifreeze, as it turns out, burns out engines if used in excess. I spent the next two hours driving circles around my block in a snowstorm, urgently expelling the antifreeze squirt by thick blue squirt. I played no music during this vigil. I couldn't find a playlist called *Poisoning Your Car*.

It may have been awkward-looking and muddled, but I was attached to my car. It was a portable home that heated my seat in winter and carried me home at night. I had no diary and rarely took pictures. That old Toyota Camry was an odd documentation of my adolescence. When I was seventeen, the car was seventeen. My younger brother entered high school last September and I passed my ownership on to him. In the weeks before I left for college, my parents made me clean it out for his sake. I spread six trash bags over the driveway, filling them with my car's contents as the August sun heated their black plastic. The task was strange, like deconstructing a scrapbook, unpeeling all the pictures and whiting out the captions.

Just like for my grandmother, it was a symbolic good-bye. Standing outside my newly vacuumed car, I wondered, if I tried hard enough, whether I could smell the Opium perfume again, or if I searched long enough, whether I'd find the matching umbrellas and the tiny sewing kit. My brother laughed at my nostalgia, reminding me that I could still drive the car when I came home. He didn't understand that it wasn't just the driving I'd miss. That it was the tinfoil balls, the *New York Times*, and the broken speaker; the fingernail marks, the stray cassettes, and the smell of chai. Alone that night and parked in my driveway, I listened to Frank Sinatra with the moon roof slid back.

Why We Care about Whales

When the moon gets bored, it kills whales. Blue whales and fin whales and humpback, sperm, and orca whales: centrifugal forces don't discriminate.

With a hushed retreat, the moon pulls waters out from under fins and flippers, oscillating them backward and forward before they slip outward. At nighttime, the moon watches its work. Silver light traces the strips of lingering water, the jittery crabs, the lumps of tangled seaweed.

Slowly, awkwardly, the whales find their footing. They try to fight the waves, but they can't fight the moon. They can't fight the world's rotation or the bathymetry of oceans or the inevitability that sometimes things just don't work out.

More than two thousand cetaceans die from beaching every year. Occasionally they trap themselves in solitude, but whales are often beached in groups, huddled together in clusters and rows. Whales feel cohesion, a sense of community, of loyalty. The distress call of a lone whale is enough to prompt its entire pod to rush to its side—a gesture that lands them nose to nose in the same sand. It's a fatal symphony of echolocation, a siren call to the sympathetic.

The death is slow. As mammals of the Cetacea order, whales are conscious breathers. Inhalation is a choice, an occasional rise to the ocean's surface. Although their ancestors lived on land, constant oxygen exposure overwhelms today's creatures.

Beached whales become frantic, captives to their hyperventilation. Most die from dehydration. The salty air shrinks their oily pores, capturing their moisture. Deprived of the buoyancy water provides, whales can literally crush themselves to death. Some collapse before they dry out—their lungs suffocating under their massive bodies—or drown when high tides cover their blowholes, filling them slowly while they're too weak to move. The average whale can't last more than twenty-four hours on land.

In their final moments, they begin belching and erupting in violent thrashing. Finally, their jaws open slightly—not all the way, but just enough that the characteristic illusion of a perpetual smile disappears. This means it's over. I know this because I watched as twenty-three whale mouths unhinged. As twenty-three pairs of whale eyes glazed over.

I had woken up that morning to a triage center outside my window. Fifty or so pilot whales were lying along the stretch of beach in front of my house on Cape Cod, surrounded by frenzied neighbors and animal activists. The Coast Guard had arrived while I was still sleeping, and guardsmen were already using boats with giant nets in an attempt to pull the massive bodies back into the water. Volunteers hurried about in groups, digging trenches around the whales' heads to cool them off, placing wet towels on their skin, and forming assembly lines to pour buckets of water on them. The energy was nervous, confused, and palpably urgent.

Pilot whales are among the most populous of the marine mammals in the cetacean order. Fully grown males can measure up to twenty feet and weigh three tons, while females usually reach sixteen feet and 1.5 tons.

Their enormity was their problem. Unlike the three dolphins that had managed to strand themselves near our house the previous summer, fifty pilot whales were nearly impossible to maneuver. If unfavorable tidal currents and topography unite, the larger species may be trapped. Sandbars sneak up on them, and the tides tie them back.

People are strange about animals. Especially large ones. Daily, on the docks of Wellfleet Harbor, thousands of fish are scaled, gutted, and seasoned with thyme and lemon. No one strokes their sides with water. No one cries when their jaws slip open.

Pilot whales are not an endangered species, yet people spend tens of thousands of dollars in rescue efforts, trucking the wounded to aquariums and in some places even airlifting them off beaches. Perhaps the whales' sheer immensity fosters sympathy. Perhaps the stories of Jonah or Moby Dick do the same. Or maybe it's that article we read last week about that whale in Australia understanding hand signals. Intelligence matters, doesn't it? Brain size is important, right? Those whales knew they were dying. They have some sort of language, some sort of emotion. They give birth, for God's sake! There aren't any pregnant fish in the Wellfleet nets. No communal understanding of their imminent fatality.

I worry sometimes that humans are afraid of helping humans. There's less risk associated with animals, less fear of failure, fear of getting too involved. In war movies, a thousand soldiers can die gruesomely, but when the horse is shot, the audience is heartbroken. It's the *My Dog Skip* effect. The *Homeward Bound* syndrome.

When we hear that the lady on the next street over has cancer, we don't see the entire town flock to her house. We push and shove and wet whales all day, then walk home through town past homeless men curled up on benches—washed up like whales on the curbsides. Pulled outside by the moon and struggling for air among the sewers. They're suffocating too, but there's no town assembly line of food. No palpable urgency, no airlifting plane.

Fifty stranded whales are a tangible crisis with a visible solution. There's camaraderie in the process, a *Free Willy* fantasy, an image of Flipper in everyone's mind. There's nothing romantic about waking up a man on a park bench and making him walk to a shelter. Little self-righteous fulfillment comes from sending a check to Oxfam International.

Would there be such a commotion if a man washed up on the beach? Yes. But stranded humans don't roll in with the tide—they hide in the corners and the concrete houses and the plains of exotic countries we've never heard of, dying of diseases we can't pronounce.

In theory I can say that our resources should be concentrated on saving human lives, that our SAVE THE WHALES T-shirts should read SAVE THE STARVING ETHIOPIANS. Logically, it's an easy argument to make. Why do we spend so much time caring about animals? Yes, their welfare is important, but surely that of humans is more so.

Last year a nonprofit spent $10,000 transporting a whale to an aquarium in Florida, where it died only three days after arriving. That same $10,000 could have purchased hundreds of thousands of food rations. In theory, this is easy to say.

But when I was looking in the eye of a dying pilot whale at four in the morning, my thoughts were not so philosophical. Four hours until high tide. Keep his skin moist. Just three hours now. There wasn't time for logic. My rationality had slipped away with the ebbing dance of the waves.

I had helped all day. We had managed to save twenty-seven of the fifty whales, but twenty-three others were deemed too far up shore, too old, or already too close to death. That night, after most of the volunteers had gone home, I went back outside my bedroom to check on the whales.

It was mid-tide, and the up-shore seaweed still crunched under my bare feet. The water was rising. The moonlight drifted down on the salt-caked battlefield, reflected in the tiny pools of water and half-shell oysters.

It was easy to spot the living whales. Their bodies, still moist, shone in the moonlight. I weaved between carcasses, kneeling down beside an old whale that was breathing deeply and far too rapidly for a healthy pilot.

I put my hands on his nose and placed my face in front of his visible eye. I knew he was going to die, and he knew he was going to die, and we both understood that there was nothing either of us could do about it.

Beached whales die on their sides, one eye pressed into the sand, the other facing up and forced to look at the moon, at the orb that pulled the water out from under its fins.

There's no echolocation on land. I imagined dying slowly next to my mother or a lover, helplessly unable to relay my parting message. I remember trying to convince myself that everything would be fine. But he wouldn't be fine. Just like the homeless man and the Ethiopian aren't fine.

Perhaps I should have been comforting one of them, placing my hands on their shoulders. Spending my time and my money and my life saving those who walked on two legs and spoke without echoes.

The moon pulled the waters forward and backward, then inward and around my ankles. Before I could find an answer, the whale's jaw unclenched, opening slightly around the edges.

Against the Grain

On my deathbed, I will instruct a nurse to bring me the following: a box of Oreos, a bag of Goldfish, a McDonald's hamburger, an assortment of Dunkin' Donuts, a chicken pot pie, a Hot Pocket, a large pepperoni pizza, a French crepe, and an ice-cold beer. In my final moments, I will consume this food slowly and delicately as I fade to oblivion. I'll start with the donuts, lemon glazed and Boston Kreme, biting at each collapsible calorie as my relatives sigh and sign condolence cards. Next, I'll sample the pizza and beer, happily slurping both as the doctors sew me up and take sad notes. "Oh," they'll say in deep baritones, "I think it's too late. I think it's the end." Everyone will gather around me, crying softly and clutching each other, as I reach gloriously for the four-cheese Hot Pocket and Big Mac Supreme.

I'm allergic to stuff. Bread, pasta, cereal, pancakes, soy sauce, seitan, hydrolyzed amp-isostearoyl, triticum mono-coccum, hordeum vulgare extract, the list goes on. Eventually, it stops at a single word—a single little protein that lurks inside ingredients at the depths of unpronounceable obscurity. Gluten. The king of all polypeptide chains. The enemy of my existence and the hero of my deathbed feast. It hides in sauces and stews, artificial colors and flavors. It teems inside deliciousness to sneak down into my small intestine and kill all my villi.

It's called Celiac Disease: an autoimmune disorder manifested in an intolerance to the proteins found in wheat, rye, barley, and other common grains. Upon exposure to gluten, my enzyme tissue transglutaminase modifies the protein, and the immune system cross-reacts with the small-bowel tissue, causing an inflammatory reaction that truncates the intestine lining and prevents nutrient absorption. In other words, my white blood cells freak out and attack the stuff like it's a virus, destroying the intestinal battlefield I unwillingly provide.

My mother taught me words like *transglutaminase* a few years after she saved my life. As a baby, I spent weeks puzzling doctors and specialists with my stick-thin limbs and distended stomach. I couldn't gain weight and threw up almost everything I ate. A test called a barium swallow finally revealed that my entire stomach had pushed into my chest, resulting in an emergency surgery to correct this hiatal hernia. Yet I stayed pale and ailing. Instead of improving, I slipped into malnourishment and was carried home from appointment after appointment to high chairs strewn with Cheerios, Saltines, and other plain poisons. My mother, devoid of expert answers, sought her own in the stacks of Boston's best libraries. She pored over pages and symptoms and Latinate labels until she found an answer under the alphabet's third letter. "Test her," she demanded to the mob of white coats. They did. She was right. And at eighteen months, I ate my first rice cake.

* * *

If Celiac Disease were an obscure Indie band, I could brag that I knew about it before everyone else. These days, GLU-

TEN FREE! is stamped upon cardboard and cupcakes from Whole Foods to local cafés. Apparently, I'm super trendy. I'm the new vegan. I'm the hip new diet that's sweeping San Francisco and Williamsburg. *Glamour* magazine prints gluten-free recipes and the *Daily Beast* featured an article last summer on its popularity among Hollywood stars. I think they're crazy. Nevertheless, I welcome the awareness. When I was diagnosed in 1990, hardly anyone had heard of the thing. This year the gluten-free market hit $2.6 billion—a number expected to double by 2015. This rice-based explosion has origins from nutritionists in Sweden to doctors in New York . . . but one such source traces closer to home.

My brothers like to tease my mom that she's obsessed with Celiac Disease. But she kind of is. She bakes endless batches of wheat-free cookies and breads, pouring them at me from ovens and pans, in the morning and in the mail. She often sends me e-mails about some newly safe product. "Rice Chex are gluten free!!!!!!!" she'll type in the message—more excited than I could ever be over tiny crisp squares. In anticipation of Passover (the most hilarious holiday), my mom counts down the days like it's the Advent, eagerly awaiting the sudden proliferation of flourless foods. I roll my eyes while half my school agonizes over the deprived horror of a week without bread, but my mom's off at distant supermarkets, hunting the best and brightest kosher cakes.

Yet above all this, she insists on vigilance. Gluten is hiding everywhere in everything, and even the tiniest crumb—the tiniest crumb of a crumb—could get me sick. It's more important than the mere stomach issues; failure to follow a gluten-free diet grossly increases one's chances of developing thyroid cancer, diabetes, and other life-threatening diseases. These, she taught me, are the real reasons to check and double-check.

The reasons she uses separate pasta strainers and knives. I learned to read labels for hidden ingredients, to call the company and ask the source of the caramel color and the modified food starch. To avoid foods fried in the same oil that had fried breaded meat. To speak with chefs at restaurants and ask to use a clean part of the grill, a clean salad bowl, a flourless dressing. We were careful. We were the best. And at home I never, ever got sick.

It wasn't easy. When I was in elementary school, my mom got fed up with the lack of resources for parents with newly diagnosed children and decided to take matters into her own hands. Working with doctors in the gastroenterology unit, my English-major mom founded Boston Children's Hospital's Celiac Support Group. She had left her job to raise my brothers and me, but her home office desk soon reemerged from my dad's papers. She built the group from the ground up, hosting meetings that turned into conferences, memos that turned into newsletters. She became the local expert on the derivatives of malt vinegar and the minutiae of cross-contamination. Inevitably, I became a Celiac poster child. I wrote advice columns and hosted an educational video. "It's not a big deal," I'd say to pitying adults or whining peers. "It's just food. It's not a big deal."

The thing is, it sort of was.

* * *

Growing up, I liked standing out. I wore rainbow pajama pants to school and acted in class plays, sang solos in assemblies and always raised my hand. I had a calm confidence that followed me through elementary and middle school—straightening my hair and holding the hand of my prepubescent boyfriend. At lunch I sat with *those* girls (eyeliner and lip gloss), shrieking like the rest of them and stealing boys' hats. We all loved attention, but when it came to the food on our fake wooden tables, I wanted nothing more than to blend into the crowd.

By sixth grade, brown bags had been discarded for Styrofoam trays. Home-packed lunches were reserved for the kids with duck boots or Power Ranger shirts. But each afternoon I pulled out a thick black thermos, filled to the steaming brim with gluten-free spaghetti or soup. Sometimes my mom packed me rice-cake sandwiches or boiled artichokes and I'd eat them quickly to fend off the endless string of embarrassing questions. *Why are you eating that? What is that weird cracker? Will I catch your thing if I share your drink?* Most of these I could shrug off with a laugh and a joke. One question, however, had no easy answer, and I dreaded its repetitions like the inevitable crumble of my dry bread.

Hey, what happens when you eat wheat?

Diarrhea. But I never told them that.

* * *

My mom did anything and everything to save me from these moments. Yet her earnest insistence on equality often left me embarrassed. On school field trips, she would call ahead to my teachers, dropping off a gluten-free cone I could have when the class stopped for ice cream. "Marina!" the teacher would call out from the front of the bus. "Come get the special ice cream cone your mom dropped off!" At home that night I'd yell across our kitchen's floors, Why would you do that? Why wouldn't you ask? Why do you always embarrass me? She'd stand there, wide-eyed, hurt. "I thought you might like a cone," she'd say. "I know you like cones with your ice cream."

Thanksgiving was the same. To ensure my experience was separate but equal, she'd bake two versions of each pie: pumpkin, apple, and chocolate pecan. Rather than be grateful, I'd sulk throughout my family gathering, embarrassed and guilty. My uncle Jim always commented on the pies: "Three gluten-free pies! You spoiled girl!" I'd seethe and blush, turning back into the kitchen to cut carrots or fold fancy napkins. There was no escaping it. Summer camp and sleepovers were the same routine—counselors and parents embarrassing me with special snacks tucked away by my mom.

On my first Halloween trick-or-treating, she called ahead to all our neighbors to make sure they had a candy I could eat, offering M&Ms and Skittles as two safe examples. It must have taken hours for her to call each family and elderly man, but all I could do was complain when six years later our block was still known as Celiac Street. "Don't bother," my friends would laugh when we were older and on a mission, lugging pillowcases instead of plastic pumpkin bins. "All we'll get are stupid M&Ms."

Yet I never *identified*. I never defined myself by my allergy to wheat. I'd respond to letters in my column from kids who felt restricted and upset, afraid to travel or go on a dinner date. "It's just food," I'd write, again and again. "It doesn't matter, it's really just food." I didn't want three special pies or an ice cream cone—all I wanted was to blend in and move on with my life. I saw the sincerity behind my mother's gestures, but it all seemed excessive, uncalled for. She'd be halfway through researching whether the canned tuna fish was gluten-free before I could remind her that I hated its saltiness. I'd laugh at her love and scoff at her efforts. It didn't matter to me. I was still too young to try on her shoes.

* * *

Before I left for college, my mother insisted on contacting dining services to research what I could and couldn't eat. She called companies and inquired about ingredients, compiling lengthy lists of foods that were and were not safe. But when I got to Yale, the lists got lost in all the novelty. I'd forget to consult them and stuck with the basics. Rice, chicken, vegetables, meat. There were new things to worry about: how to play beer pong without beer, how not to French-kiss a boy after his late-night pizza. When I finished my freshman year five pounds lighter, my mom looked worried and asked about the lists. I confessed that they were too hard to follow, and the summer before my sophomore fall, she sought to fully transform Yale's food-allergy plan. With her credentials from Boston Children's Hospital, she arranged meetings with our head chefs and supervisors, getting gluten-free cereals and bagels in dining halls, adding "gluten" labels on every dish's information cards. It was unbelievable. It was impressive. Watching her make calls, I could see her eyes smile with the smallest hint of pride.

* * *

My junior year, I moved off campus. And with this departure came a farewell to the campus meal plan. I dismissed the hours and efforts as I had the cones and pies. I wanted to live in a house. I wanted a bigger bed. I was annoyed at the guilt I felt at leaving. After all, I hadn't *asked* her to put in all that work. Miraculously, still, her efforts annoyed me. She'd arrive at Yale with six bags of groceries, lugging three kinds of gluten-free pretzels upstairs.

On vacations, I'd gain weight. From the moment my car crunched my driveway's thick ice to the moment I'd pile back into my aging sedan, I'd be presented with feasts every meal of the day. I hated it. Too guilty to refuse, I'd be forced to eat my weight in gluten-free goods. Plans to run every day and cut college's convenience-store pounds were thwarted each winter and spring by her earnest offerings. On a warm Saturday this April, I awoke to a massive pile of blueberry pancakes. I was still full from the previous night's chicken curry, and the sight of the plate finally forced me to crack. My mother stood silently as I cruelly complained she was making me fat. "Stop feeding me, Mom," I said with a cold exasperation. "How the hell am I supposed to stay thin when you feed me all this damn food?" Compulsively accommodating, she apologized for her hours of labor, her chocolate-chip banana muffins, her walnut fudge brownies. She moved my plate to the sink and retreated to her office, leaving me near tears in a kitchen that still smelled of baked maple, shamefully eating a yogurt and going upstairs.

* * *

A year later, I'm loose with my diet. I take risks, I forget to double-check. At restaurants, I don't bother talking to the chef; in my kitchen, I'm too lazy to drain my pasta in its own colander. I kiss my boyfriend after he's had a beer; I neglect to check when caramel color is involved. My physical symptoms have largely subsided, and any trace amount of gluten in my blood affects me mostly in the vague statistical increase of my chances for cancer. I don't think about my red blood cell count when I eat cheese off plates that might have touched crackers. I'm young. I'm fine. It's just food, I say, again and again. It doesn't matter, it's really just food.

* * *

On a cold morning this past February, my family went out for brunch the day after my play. We went to a place on Chapel Street, trudging through plow piles and slush into its elegant doors. I was happy to be with my mother, to talk and to hug. I'd had a difficult month with rooming dramas and summer plans, and it was nice to relax in the comfort of family. When it was time to order, I requested a vegetable omelet and roasted potatoes to replace the home fries. "I'm allergic to gluten," I added after my order. "It should be fine but you can let the chef know." I could feel my mom eyeing me over the winter flowers. She managed to restrain herself until our orange juice came in thin brittle glasses.

"Marina, honey," she began, "did you want to ask the chef to cook your eggs on a clean griddle?"

"Not really." I played with my fork.

"Well, what about the oil they use for roasting?" I knew she didn't want to pester me, didn't want to mother her daughter who was now twenty-one.

"Mom, it's fine. There's a ninety-nine-point-nine percent chance it's fine."

But that was never enough.

* * *

On a rainy March middle of the night, I was lost in my laptop when I stumbled across an article online. I was trying to search what types of vodka are gluten-free, but what I found instead was a study on pregnancy and the gluten-free diet. New findings, it said, found that gluten can harm the development of a Celiac's unborn child. Even the tiniest presence, it said, can affect the baby's ability to absorb enough nutrients. I read the article twice and turned down my iTunes. I was struck in that moment with the absolute conviction that someday, when I was pregnant, I would be insanely careful. I'd eat only at home, boiling brown rice and vegetables—call every company on every ingredient, checking, double-checking, and checking again. Then I started crying.

* * *

My mother and I were watching old family videos one summer on our living-room TV when we came across the footage of my first birthday party. I'm sitting in a high chair with a pointy paper hat, and my family and friends are gathered around, laughing and waving. Soon the lights dim and my mother walks in—a younger, longer-haired mother with full cheeks and bright eyes. Illuminating her face and the tiny dining room is a glorious birthday cake with flaming Mickey Mouse candles. "Happy birthday to you," they sing. "Happy birthday to you." But my real-life mother, my older, thinner mother, had her hand clutched over her mouth, glassy-eyed and fixed on the screen.

"I'm poisoning you," she whispered, shaking her head. "I'm poisoning you, Marina. I'm poisoning you." I went to the VCR and turned off the footage.

"It's okay, Mom," I said. But she was already shaken.

I was reminded in that moment of the stories my father told about my infant months spent in hospitals and waiting rooms. He'd urge my mother to sleep at home or in the visitor ward, but she wouldn't listen. Each and every night she slept upright, propped uncomfortably in hospital-room chairs.

* * *

Nineteen years later, I lie in my too-big New Haven bed, aimless and sleepless. I go on Facebook. I check my e-mail. I think back to the M&Ms and the sleepover snacks, the field-trip cones and the Thanksgiving pies. The thousands of brownies she baked and the phone calls she made. I think of blueberry pancakes and vegetable omelets, hospital beds and my first birthday cake. I read the article again before I turn off my light. When I'm pregnant, I think, I'll eat just boiled rice.

Putting the "Fun" Back in Eschatology

I f you didn't already know this, the sun is going to die.
When I think about the future, I don't think about ines-
capable ends. But even if we solve global warming and destroy
nuclear bombs and control population, ultimately the human
race will annihilate itself if we stay here. Eventually, inevitably,
we will no longer be able to live on Earth: we have a giant fire-
ball clock ticking down twilight by twilight.

In many ways, I think mortality is more manageable when
we consider our eternal components, our genetics and oth-
erwise that carry on after us. Still, soon enough, the books
we write and the plants we grow will freeze up and rot in the
darkness.

But maybe there's hope.

What the universe really boils down to is whether a planet
evolves a life-form intelligent enough to create technology
capable of transporting and sustaining that life-form off the
planet before the sun in that planet's solar system explodes. I
have a limited set of comparative data points, but I'd estimate
that we're actually doing okay at this point. We already have
(intelligent) life, technology, and (primitive) space travel. And

we still have some time before our sun runs out of hydrogen and goes nuclear.

Yet none of that matters unless we can develop a sustainable means of living and traveling in space. Maybe we can. What I've concluded is that if we do reach this point, we have crossed a remarkable threshold—and will emerge into the (rare?) evolutionary status of having outlived the very life source that created us.

It's natural selection on a Universal scale. "The Origin of the Aliens," one could say; a survival of the fittest planets. Planets capable of evolving life intelligent enough to leave before the lights go out. I suppose that without a God, NASA is my anti-nihilism. Alone and on my laptop, these ideas can humble me into apathy. My sophomore year's juxtaposition of Galaxies and the Universe with Introduction to International Relations made the latter seem laughably small in scale.

But I had this thought the other night. My instinct, of course, is to imagine us as one of many planets racing its evolution against its sun—merely one in the galactic Darwinian pursuit. But maybe we're not. Maybe all this talk of the inevitability of aliens is garbage and we're miraculously, beautifully alone in our biological success. What if we're winning? What if we're actually the most evolved intelligence in all this big bang chaos? What if other planets have bacteria and single-celled genotypes but nothing more?

The precedent is all the more pressing. Humans alone could be winning the race against our giant gas time bomb and running with the universal Olympic torch. What an honor. What a responsibility. What a gift we have been given to be born in an atmosphere with oxygen and carbon dioxide and millions of years and phenotypes cheering us on with recycles of energy.

The thing is, I think we can make it. I think we can shove ourselves into spaceships before things get too cold.

I only hope we don't fuck things up before that. Because millions of years is a long time and I don't want to let the universe down.

I Kill for Money

Tommy Hart swings a dead mouse back and forth by its tail and grins.

"Ooo, a *corpus delicti,* how deeelectable," he coos, popping up from under the sink and licking his lips. "Rodent *à la carte* anyone?" Tommy bursts into laughter at his own joke, his blue eyes bulging with excitement as he examines the recently trap-squashed mouse. It's 9:30 in the morning at Larry's Lakeside Diner in Chicago, and with three dead mice already stiffly huddled in his black pouch, Tommy is in a good mood. "And this, my friends," he proclaims to the four young chefs crowded near him, "is why they call me Dr. Death." He pauses, glances around, then begins to hum the theme song from *Jaws.* Even for a sixty-three-year-old exterminator, Thomas H. Hart is a bit odd.

"I don't know whether to be happy you're catching 'em, or pissed 'cause you keep finding more," says a tall, unshaven man with a stamped nametag that reads HEAD CHEF. He watches with baffled amusement as his exterminator prowls the kitchen floor on hands and knees. For the past year, Larry's Diner has been "having a bit of a problem" with mice. Larry called Tommy about two months ago, and he's been coming every week since.

"Larry, Larry," replies Tommy, pulling his old jeans up with one hand as he glances toward him, "your kitchen will be *squeaky* clean in no time." Tommy's head falls back down as he lets out a stream of wheezy laughter.

Despite the early hour, the cluttered kitchen of Larry's Diner is somewhat dim. A stream of yellow light pours out of Tommy's foot-long metallic flashlight as he jerks it between economy-size jars of mayonnaise to check the rest of his pre-laid mousetraps. The floor is in desperate need of a mop. A sour marshy smell creeping in from the nearby lake hovers in the air and provides a fitting environment for Tommy's some-what nautical appearance. Tommy chooses to wear a Greek fisherman's hat with a metal bonefish pinned to the front simply because it "feels right." His gray curly hair crawls out from the edges of his hat, framing his face—a by-product of thousands of laugh lines. He's tan, and he has deep-set eyes, bushy gray eyebrows, and a walrus mustache. A red, yellow, blue, and green striped sweater is visible under his black wind-breaker jacket with the word BEEFEATER printed across the left breast.

Tommy's been in the exterminating business for about forty years. "Bugs, mice, rats, squirrels, birds; you name it, I'll kill it." Tommy beams. "Why stop?" He shrugs. "I just love it." Although he used to work for a pest control company in Evanston, when the building was seized by the Internal Revenue Service, he decided to start his own business with one of his coworkers, Chris O'Leary. "We split up our accounts and took everything fifty-fifty. Real nice guy, O'Leary. Start-ing that up was the best thing that has ever happened to me." Tommy's face sags out of his smile as he adds, "My partner died a few years ago, though." Less comfortable in a serious atmosphere, Tommy quickly changes the mood. "He died of hemorrhagic pneumonia. It's a virus, you know, so a *bug* finally got him back." He grins broadly, but the smile doesn't quite make it into his eyes.

"Hey, Tommy, I'm going to go shovel the walkway," yells Larry from the customer section of the restaurant. "Call me if you need the key to the maintenance closet."

"Si, señor," Tommy shouts back, opening up his dark green toolbox, where he keeps supplies. Holding the flashlight in his teeth, Tommy takes out a series of new Victor mousetraps and sticky paper-baiting sheets. He hums unmelodiously to himself as his rough hands open and set a mousetrap with one swift and fearless motion. "Here's my card," he jokes, holding out the rectangular trap and speaking in a sleazy car-salesman voice. "I run a real *snappy* business." Tommy cracks up again as he opens a different compartment of the toolbox and retrieves his secret mouse bait: Slim Jims. He explains that the pungent odor and sticky texture are perfect for the traps; he laughs, "Hell, why not give those suckers high cholesterol while we're at it?" Crawling on his hands and knees, Tommy checks under shelves and behind the giant ovens, peering wide-eyed for any signs of "black rice," his euphemism for mouse and rat poop.

The pest control industry has changed a lot since Tommy started into it some forty years ago. "A lot of the chemicals and equipment and stuff that we use and the way we approach pest control is completely different now." Tommy squints, peers under the giant refrigerator, and bends closer to the concrete floor. "Another little guy, Jesus! They must love Larry's cooking," he proclaims, leaning down to unclasp the dead gray mouse. With his purple latex surgeon's gloves (which he finds more exciting than clear ones), Tommy examines the body of his victim with glowing eyes before plopping him into his bag. "Anyway," he continues, "the buzzword now is IPM: Integrated Pest Management. IPM is basically a way of approaching pest control which utilizes chemical treatment as a last resort; in other words, educating people on how to seal things"—he pauses for a moment as he wipes the dried blood off the used trap—"how to do things in a more environmentally friendly manner, how to use sanitation and block holes. It's all about not creating situations conducive to animals and insects entering into homes."

Tommy, however, probably wouldn't mind rodents or beetles wandering into his house. His interest in extermination harks back to a childhood fascination with bugs and the natural world. "That stuff doesn't scare me at all. I was introduced to the outdoors at an early age and was very interested by everything. I used to collect bugs and put them in little jars." Tommy wrinkles his mustache up and down and widens his eyes. "At summer camp my friends and I used to play with snakes. We used to catch frogs in the pond and watch the snakes eat them alive headfirst."

Actually dealing with the creatures and doing the real grungy physical work is what Tommy loves most about his job. "When I started in the business, I worked as an exterminator for about six months and then they promoted me inside the office to do paperwork and other things. I mean, I got more money for it, but I just couldn't take it. Some people are money driven; some aren't." Tommy pauses and resets the trap. "I like the satisfaction of solving people's problems. That's the most rewarding thing by far."

Tommy pushes himself up onto his feet. He breathes in deeply, then exhales in a quick burst as he straightens his sailor's hat and brings his left hand up to salute. "On to My Lai!" Tommy orders. "The enemy lies ahead!" He marches over to the maintenance closet door and sets his green toolbox down with a clank. "Hmm, hmm, hmm," he hums, tilting his head back and forth, "door key, shmore key." With a swift motion he flicks open the blade of a rusted Swiss Army Knife and slides it through the crack between the door and wall. "Voilà," Tommy beams, and the door clicks open instantly.

"I tend to use sticky paper bait pads in closets," he explains as he makes his way into the shelf-lined room. "When people walk in, it's usually pretty dark, and we wouldn't want their toes getting snapped off, now would we?" He grins. "The mice wander onto the pad, and their noses and feet get stuck. After break-dancing for about ten minutes they settle down and suffocate to death, 'cause they can't breathe." He shuts the closet door behind him and switches on his flashlight, eerily illuminating his face from below. "Do *youuu* like to break-dance, my dear?" Tommy flicks on the closet bulb, his laughter echoing in the small room.

Tommy acknowledges that most people are very uncomfortable with bugs and vermin and knows that his humor serves to calm them down, claiming that "his lighthearted nature helps his business." However, Tommy's sense of humor has not always been an asset. "See, I almost got kicked out of the first company I worked for. I was assigned to give a thirty- to forty-five-minute discussion on bat control, and as I approached the podium, I had a wooden hammer, three wooden stakes, a black cloak, and a copy of the Old Testament." He wheezes, then stops to collect himself. "God, I thought that was just hilarious. Too bad my boss didn't."

Although Tommy's customers all agree that he's a funny guy, some of them admit he sometimes takes it too far in mocking himself. "Tommy's a riot," Larry says, "but sometimes I feel like he's laughing at his own profession so that others won't. I mean, he's great, don't get me wrong. It's just that I get the feeling he's a bit embarrassed." Larry looks over both his shoulders before continuing in a hushed voice. "I mean, look at his truck. No markings, nothing. Just plain white. He'll joke about it, but there's no giant cockroach painted on the back."

Even Tommy understands that he sometimes hides behind his jokes. "For the most part people perceive me as I perceive myself, but there are times when people have been rude to me." He pauses, starts to say something different, then stops. His body tenses up and he begins to rub his hands as if washing them in invisible water. "I mean, I guess you could say I sometimes use humor as a defense mechanism." He stops again, as if thinking over whether or not he really does. "There are all different types of people and issues that you have to deal with when you work in a job like this. Some people approach you very nicely. Some people, well, some people don't." He shrugs and shakes his head, averting his eyes. "Some people are different, very judgmental."

Tommy fingers the fish pin on his cap, then awkwardly laughs. "Well, the roach coach is calling!" he proclaims, referencing his nickname for his truck. "I got a nasty case of bedbugs to deal with over in Washington Heights and this kitchen is *squeaky* clean for now." He guffaws, apparently unaware of his joke's repetition. Although Tommy seems clueless, Larry admits his repertoire of jokes is like "a sitcom on rerun." Gathering his stuff, Tommy trudges out the back door of the diner and into the cold Chicago air.

Tommy's old unlabeled truck is parked perfectly in one of the many open spaces. Despite its white, spotless shell, the inside of Tommy's vehicle is a reflection of his unique personality. The back of the truck serves as a storage room for traps, nets, gloves, structural repair items, sticky boards, pheromone traps, sprays, and more than twelve different kinds of poison. The front is subject to a series of bumper stickers stuck to the inside walls for only Tommy to see. Ironically, most of them seem to shout things at other drivers. HORN BROKEN. WATCH FOR FINGER, one reads. BEWARE: RED GREEN COLOR CONFU-SION, boasts another. A small stuffed parrot hangs from the rearview mirror, squawking things like *"Let me see your tits!"* and *"Polly wants a fucking cracker!"* when squeezed. On the driver's side, the decor is more serious. THE SERVICE INDUS-TRY MEANS SERVICE reads one sticker. A 1/20/09: BUSH'S FINAL DAY sticker is stuck just inches away from one that reads NOT ANOTHER VIETNAM: STOP WAR IN IRAQ.

As a liberal Democrat, Tommy has always been against war. However, in the winter of 1967, at the age of twenty-two, he was drafted into the U.S. Army. Up until then, Tommy had had a difficult time finding his place in society. He attended four different schools: North Shore Country Day, Notre Dame, Deerfield High School, and Culver Academy in Indiana—one for each year of high school. *"Magna cum laude* were three words I never heard in my education," he chuck-les. "I wasn't the world's greatest student." After graduat-ing, Tommy attended college in San Francisco, where he was introduced to the "whole sixties thing." He explains, "When I was living out in California, I became pretty friendly with this hippie colony that lived near campus. I remember telling one of the guys there that I had just got drafted. I mean, I could have run to Canada and hidden out, but that's just not me. I just couldn't do it.".

Although he served in the army from 1967 to 1970, Tommy never actually had to go to Vietnam. As one of only two hun-dred enlisted men to avoid the war, Tommy was deployed to a small town in Germany where he was assigned to watch over things as a ski patrolman. "I'm a Vietnam *era* vet, not an actual Vietnam vet. Some guy in a computer punching numbers, that's all it was. I was damn lucky, that's for sure. I just got to ski around. Hah! Pretty good way to spend my duty." Tommy breathes in deeply and sighs. "Anyway, that's the past. Unimportant now for the most part, other than the fact that they made me cut off my hair. I had an Afro back then. I mean, I still have a lot of hair. I'm sixty-three, and look at all this shit." Tommy grabs two clumps of his gray curls and pulls them outward. "I don't look sixty-three, I don't feel sixty-three, I don't act sixty-three, and I don't care. Age is but a state of mind, my dear." After a long pause, Tommy becomes uncomfortable in his own seriousness and jerks his head quickly to the left, breaking eye contact. "Ha! Did I ever tell you my friends call me Dr. Death? That's more important. Write that down, my dear, write that down."

Tommy starts up his truck and begins to drive away from the windy harbor and south toward Washington Heights. On an average day, Tommy makes about five or six stops, which usually take somewhere between six and ten hours. His customers include big businesses, office buildings, schools, restaurants, and residential homes. He likes to organize his day so that he starts in the city and works his way back out to the suburbs and toward his home, where he raised his two children and now lives alone with his wife, Janice.

Tommy's wife admires his passion for small creatures. However, she admits that he can be "a bit obsessive" at times. "I'll come downstairs to get some water at like one in the morning, and he'll be sitting there all excited over some *Nova* program on the Discovery Channel about spider mating, or cockroach burrowing techniques." She stops, smiles slightly, and fingers a wine-colored birthmark on her left cheek. "It's not so much the bug obsession as it is all those jokes. Oh, Lord, day in and day out, and he's his own biggest fan when it comes to humor. Cracks himself up nearly every minute."

Tommy has a different perspective on his marriage. "The insect society is matriarchal. That is, the queen is the supreme ruler." He chuckles. "That's different in my house, though. My philosophy towards my wife is: 'The daily beatings will continue until morale improves.'" He cracks his knuckles by pressing his hands together but then quickly holds them up on either side of his head in a gesture of surrender. "I'm joking, I'm joking," he laughs. "Oh, man, I could tell you a million jokes, a hundred million jokes if you wanted. Hey, so what do you get when you cross a centipede and a parrot? . . . A walkie-talkie!" He throws his head back and lets out a loud wheeze.

Tommy takes a sip from a Mister Donut coffee as he flicks on the radio and starts swaying his head back and forth to a smooth jazz song. He takes a sharp left and pulls up next to a run-down concrete apartment complex of about five stories. Colorful graffiti surrounds the lower level of the building and a large white banner hangs over the entrance that reads APARTMENTS FOR RENT: CALL 773-555-0962 FOR MORE INFORMATION. Tommy takes one last sip of his coffee, and with a twist of his wrist, the car turns off and the music goes silent. "Welcome to the derelict city," Tommy says in a mock low voice. "Gateway to downtown ghetto."

The landlord called Tommy a few days ago, desperately begging him to come "as soon as he possibly could" to deal with a bedbug problem in one of the apartments he's trying to rent. "Bedbugs are becoming more and more of an issue these days," Tommy explains as he retrieves his supplies from the back of the truck. They resemble little black ticks that live in the cracks and springs of mattresses and rely on human blood for food. The key to knowing you have a problem, Tommy describes, is seeing little red spots all over the bed. "It's their feces," he laughs harshly. "Disgusting, huh?" He walks over piles of brown snow toward the back door of the complex and knocks.

A middle-aged man with a receding hairline opens the door and looks Tommy up and down.

"I take it you're the exterminator," he asserts in a thick accent.

"That's me." Tommy smiles and holds out his hand, "Thomas H. Hart: I kill for money." The landlord doesn't laugh, nor does he shake Tommy's hand.

"Like I told you on the phone, we need a bedbug spray-down in C3 on the third floor."

"Well, luckily, all I have to do is kill one bug and the rest will leave the bed to go to his funeral." Tommy bends over laughing, almost losing hold of his supplies.

"Look, I have a shitload to do before I rent these things," the landlord says coolly, adjusting his faded blue tie. "Just get the damn bugs out. If you need me, I'll be in my office."

Tommy stands still, his lips pressed tightly together. In silence, he pushes the door open and trudges up the musty staircase holding his heavy metal pesticide sprayer in his right hand. Once on the third floor, he starts posting warning signs all over the doors of the seemingly vacant building, still in an angry silence.

"Sorry about that," Tommy finally says. "Sometimes I just feel so goddamn angry at people." He forcefully takes off his sailor's hat and tucks it into his bag. He breathes in deeply and, after a pause, relaxes into a smile. "Whatever. I don't want to talk about it. No one will want to read about all my stupid emotional stuff. No one cares."

Out of a large black duffel bag, Tommy pulls a pair of thick gloves and a roll of duct tape. After taping the sleeves of his shirt and the legs of his pants closed, he slips on his gloves and wriggles his head inside a World War I–era gas mask. All suited up, Tommy is somewhere between frightening and comical. "Bloodsucking bedbugs," he muses, his voice sounding weirdly mechanical and muted through the mask's air filter. "Sounds like something out of a scary horror movie." He pauses and gestures to his eccentric appearance. "But then again, look at me. I suppose I'd fit right in." He half smiles.

"On to My Lai!" Tommy suddenly declares. "The enemy lies ahead!" He brings his left hand up to salute and marches into the dusty, vacated apartment. A single window provides the light for the room, and with its low ceiling, dank smell, and sheet-covered furniture, the atmosphere is reminiscent of an old attic. Alone in the left corner of the room, a queen-size mattress lies like a victim, exposed and bare except for a few mysterious stains. Tommy places the heavy B&G chemical sprayer down on the old wood floor, laughing that he has no idea what the two initials stand for. The machine resembles an oddly sized scuba tank: a one-and-a-half-foot metal cylinder with three red nozzles protruding from its top surface. In the middle of these three sprayers is a gold pump used both to increase pressure of the spray and to reload new poisons. Moving closer to the bed, Tommy loads the enzyme pesticide into the tank and pumps the machine's gold lever down about ten times before grabbing one of the red tubes and bringing it over to the bare mattress. "I can't believe I'm still doing this at sixty-three." Tommy laughs. "Did I tell you I'm sixty-three? I don't think I did. I don't look sixty-three, I don't feel sixty-three, I don't act sixty-three, and I don't care."

Tommy's daughter, Anna, who now lives in Arizona, explains, "I usually call home about once a week, and Dad will sometimes tell me the same story twice in one phone call." She pauses. "I mean, he's always been like that with jokes, but now it's other stuff too." She stops again, then laughs slightly. "I don't really understand why he's still working. Forty years . . . Forty years killing bugs and rats. Well, it sure beats me."

Growing up with an exterminator as a father was always slightly embarrassing for Anna and her brother, Kevin. "I remember," Tommy begins, "one year when Anna was about eight, and it was 'bring your daughter to work day.' That was a big thing back in the eighties," he chuckles. "Well, I remember Anna came down to breakfast that morning and told me she didn't want to come." Tommy half smiles, but shakes his head slightly and closes his eyes for a second. "'Dad-*dyyy*, bugs are nasty. Why can't you be a pilot or a doctor or something cool like that?' I didn't even argue with her, I just let her go to school." Tommy sighs, "I told her I was sorry I didn't have a cooler job."

Moving with deliberation, Tommy slowly disinfects the bed by spraying the clear and odorless poison over the frame, edges, and then center. Peering close enough to the mattress, he can see the tiny black bedbugs writhing and shaking in agony for a few seconds before they fall still. "When I see bugs outside I never kill them. There's no real satisfaction in killing them." Tommy pauses as he watches a particularly twitchy one. Walking back and forth along the side of the bed, he switches between the three red tubes, each spraying in a different shape: fanlike, mist, and jet. "All insects and rodents and stuff play a part in Mother Nature's scheme of things. It's a balancing act. I mean, I could technically get arrested for this because it's breaking the law, but when I catch squirrels in people's houses, I usually sneak them into my truck and let them free in the woods somewhere. The law says you're supposed to drown them, but I just can't do it." Tommy sighs and shuts off the machine, a new silence hovering in the room. "That should do," he proclaims, standing back to observe his work, then walking over toward the wall next to the bed. Through his fogged-up gas mask, Tommy's blue eyes gaze out the frosted window at the street below. Moving closer, he presses his hands up against the cold glass, cooling them off from the heat of the machine. "I don't know," Tommy sighs. "I just don't know."

Tommy suddenly picks up his stuff and starts walking down the stairs. "I'm honest, I'm never late, I respect people, I try my hardest, I'm friendly, I love my wife, I love my children," he rants as he makes his way out of the building and toward his truck. "It's just like, no one wants bugs around, so no one wants *me* around." Tommy shakes his head and shoves his supplies into the truck. "I mean, why do you think it's unlabeled?" He waves an arm outward toward his truck. "Because people would be embarrassed to have it in their parking lots, that's why." He shakes his head, suddenly stops talking, and sighs. "Ehh, stupid landlord. He's just an asshole anyway. What do I care?" Tommy smiles and his body becomes less tense. "Hey, here's one I've never told you, my dear. What do you get when you cross a centipede and a parrot? . . . A walkie-talkie!" He gags, and bends over laughing. Tommy slides into the driver's seat of his truck and shuts the door, sealing the plain white shell around him.

Even Artichokes Have Doubts

If this year is anything like the last ten, around 25 percent of employed Yale graduates will enter the consulting or finance industry. This is a big deal. This is a huge deal. This is so many people! This is one-fourth of our people! Regardless of what you think or with whom you're interviewing, we ought to be pausing for a second to ask why.

I don't pretend to know any more about this world than the rest of us. In fact, I probably know less. (According to the Internet, a consultant is "someone who consults someone or something.") But I do know that this statistic is utterly and entirely shocking to me. In a place as diverse and disparate as Yale, it's remarkable that such a large percentage of people are doing anything the same—not to mention something as significant as their postgraduate plans.

I want to understand.

* * *

In the spring of my sophomore year, I got my first e-mail from McKinsey & Company. "Dear Marina," it read, "Now that you have finished your sophomore year, I am sure that you're starting to think about what the future may have in store for you." (I hadn't.) "Perhaps you are starting to experience that nervous, exciting, overwhelming feeling that comes with exploring the options that are coming your way at Yale, especially given your involvement in the Yale College Democrats. To help you get a better sense of what is out there, I thought I would take the opportunity to provide some more insight into McKinsey & Company."

This weirded me out. How did they know I was involved with the Yale College Democrats? (How did they know about that nervous, exciting, overwhelming feeling!?) As a sophomore, I'd hardly settled on a major, let alone a career path. But despite myself, it made me feel special. Who were these people? Why were they interested in me? Why were they inviting me to events at nice hotels? Maybe I perused their website, WHO KNOWS? The point is: they got me, for at least an evening, to look into this thing and see what it was all about.

Of course, everyone gets these e-mails. I'm not special. Their team of recruiters is really good. They come to Yale with myriad other consultant firms and banks and sell themselves shamelessly and brilliantly to us from the time we turn twenty. We get e-mails and career-fair booths, letters and deadlines. I don't know much about consulting but I do know that if I were having trouble recruiting smart kids for a job, I'd hire a consulting firm to help me out.

But it's not just them. It's us, too. I conducted a credible and scientific study in L-Dub courtyard earlier this week—asking freshman after freshman what they thought they might be doing upon graduation. Not one of them said they wanted to be a consultant or an investment banker. Now, I'm sure that these people do exist—but they certainly weren't expressing interest at a rate of 25 percent. Unsurprisingly, most students don't seem to come to Yale with explicit passions for these fields. Yet sometime between Freshman Screw and the Last Chance Dance something in our collective cogs shifts and these jobs become attractive. We're told they will help us gain valuable skills. We're told a lot of things.

* * *

One senior I spoke with (whom we'll refer to as Shloe Carbib for the sake of Google anonymity) has known what she's wanted since freshman year. When asked what she hoped to do with her life, Shloe responded immediately: "Oh, you know, I want to write and direct films or be an indie music celebrity." Ironies of expression aside, there was a sincerity to her avowal. "I want to devote my life to the things that I love. I want to create something lasting that I'm really proud of."

At Yale, she's worked hard in pursuit of these goals—directing theatrical productions, playing in a band, and collaborating on the 2012 Class Day Video. Yet on Monday evening at eight P.M., she found herself at a top-tier consulting firm event at The Study, meeting and greeting in anticipation of her interview the next morning.

"Of course I don't want to be a consultant," she said the night before, clutching a borrowed copy of Marc Cosentino's *Case in Point* (the aspiring-consultant bible). "It's just very scary to watch as many of your friends have already secured six-figure salaries and are going to be living in luxury next year. I'm trying to figure out if I love art enough to be poor."

Like many students, Carbib was roped in by the easy application process. All she had to do to apply to the firm was submit a résumé, cover letter, and transcript by the drop deadline.

"Oh, it's brilliant of them to make their first round of applications so easy," she said. "It was so little work that I felt like I might as well try."

Indeed, the recruiting tactics of these companies are undeniably effective. They express interest in us personally—complimenting our intelligence and general aptitude and convincing us that those skills ought to be utilized to their full capacity (with them, of course).

Tatiana Schlossberg '12 admits she initially fell for the same trick I did.

"I got a personal e-mail and went to their event because I couldn't believe that they were interested in me and I wanted to find out why," she said. But when she got there, she wasn't sure why she'd come in the first place. "I looked around and felt that I not only didn't belong with the group of people but that I didn't believe in what the organization stands for or does," she said. "There's definitely a compulsion element to it. You feel like so many people are doing it and talking about it all the time like it's interesting, so you start to wonder if maybe it really is."

Mark Sonnenblick '12 wonders if it might be. A musician, writer, and improvisational comedian at Yale, Mark is looking into (among other things) a job at a hedge fund next year. "I want a job that will dynamically engage me," he said. "But I guess the bottom line is that I want a job in general and I don't really know how to get a job. This is easy to apply for and would make me a lot of money." Ultimately, he hopes to work writing music and plays but understands that's not exactly a field with an application form.

Of course, many of the people I talked to expressed more explicit interest in the industry. Well, to be fair, most people didn't want to say anything at all. For every student I interviewed, at least four others refused. In the age of digital print, applicants are (understandably) worried about potential employers searching their names and finding angsty quotes about Their Doubts and Their Hopes. One Saybrook senior declined an interview because he reckoned there was no way to "not sound like a douchebag." Either he'd come off as pompous for sounding excited about his future job or superior for sounding too good for it. In the words of Michael Blume '12, "They don't wanna be interviewed 'cause they already be on the path to making mad bills."

However, a few people with offers and interest were willing to talk to me. Their stories and motivations for pursuing consulting or finance had remarkable similarities. The narrative goes something like this: eventually, I want to save the world in some way. Right now, the best way for me to do that is to gain essential skills by working in this industry for a few years.

Former Yale College Council president Jeff Gordon '12 is a great example. Jeff wants to devote his life to public education policy reform but is considering a job at a hedge fund among other options for next year.

"I guess the appeal of that kind of job is more in personal development than in any content area," he said. "It's appealing because it seems challenging and because it involves interaction with smart and talented people. There are also some transferable skills." Yet Jeff claims he could not see himself working in the industry forever.

"I couldn't imagine myself doing something outside the content area that I care about for more than a few years," he added. "I take something of a long view on this—I want to place myself in a position to make a very positive difference in social justice."

But at the same time he has some doubts about these motives: "I think the last time that most of us went through something like this was when we were applying to college and we're conditioned to accept the ready-made, established process. The problem is, most places don't have something like that. It's messy and confusing and we're often afraid of dealing with that mess," he said. "Second of all, a lot of people, myself included, are very worried about narrowing their options or specializing, and consulting firms do a great job of convincing us that we still have many options open.

"I think it's a combination of that and prestige," he added.

Annie Shi '12 has similar justifications for her job at J.P. Morgan next year. When asked what she might be most interested in doing with her life, she mentioned a fantasy of opening a restaurant that supports local artists and sustainable food. Eventually, she's "aiming for something that does more good than just enriching [her]self." She just doesn't think she's ready for anything like that quite yet.

"How can I change the world as a twenty-one- or twenty-two-year-old?" she said. "I know that's a very pessimistic view, but I don't feel like I have enough knowledge or experience to step into those shoes. Even if you know that you want to go into the public sector, you'd benefit from experience in the private sector."

Annie also considers the financial incentives of the position.

"I'm practical," she says. "I'm not going to work at a non-profit for my entire life; I know that's not possible. I'm realistic about the things that I need for a lifestyle that I've become accustomed to." Though she admits she's at least partially worried about ending up at the bank "longer than [she] sees [her]self there now," at present she sees it as a "hugely stimulating and educational" way to spend the next few years.

Others disagree. One senior who interned with J.P. Morgan (and who requested anonymity) had a very different experience with the bank.

"Working there was a combination of the least fulfilling, least interesting, and least educational experiences of my life. I guess I did learn something, but I learned it in the first two days and could have stopped my internship then. In the next two months I learned nothing but still came in to work early and for some reason had to stay until ten," he said. "I would see these people who loved it, but honestly it seemed like they were either uninteresting or lying to themselves."

But Annie and Jeff weren't the only two students I spoke with who subscribed to this notion of the private sector as a kind of training ground. The industries certainly work hard to advance this idea—marketing themselves as the best and fastest way to train oneself for . . . anything.

* * *

Kevin Hicks '89, former dean of Berkeley College, thinks it's a load of crap.

"As for the argument that consulting provides an extraordinary skill set with which one can eventually change the world, I just don't buy it," he said. "Everyone knows what the skill set is for most entry-level consultants: PowerPoint and Excel." He sees a huge problem with the idea that consulting and finance are good ways to prepare oneself for a career elsewhere.

"Most firms are looking for people who will stay up until three A.M. seven nights a week making slides for a partner who goes home to Wellesley for dinner every night at five P.M.—and who will do so thinking that they're 'winning.' Look at it this way: most firms assume that you'll leave for law school or business school within three years, and they invest in your training accordingly. Quality mentoring when you're young is worth whatever you pay for it. Sometimes that means less money, sometimes that means less of a life beyond work. But quality mentoring is not going to be delivered by someone who is twenty-six, and just one tidal cycle ahead of you."

Hicks believes this idea of skill-set development is a product of fantastic marketing by the firms themselves.

"There are a half dozen more life-affirming ways you can acquire those same skills, including taking a class at night at a junior college while you do something more interesting. I suppose I'm open to the idea that consulting may truly be a great first job for someone, but too many seniors march lemming-like toward it because everyone else seems to be doing it, and it's the next opportunity for extrinsic validation. If McKinsey says you're okay, you're okay.

"The danger in doing a prefabricated thing after graduation," he continued, "is that there's no unique story to tell about it. If there was ever a moment to be entrepreneurial and daring—whether in terms of business or social change—and really test yourself, this is it.

"If you're like most people, you'll do one thing for two to three years, then something else for two to three years, and then—somewhere in that five- to seven-year distance from Yale—you'll see a need to fully commit to something that's a longer-term project: graduate school, for example, or a job you need to stick with for some real time. The question is: where do you need to be with yourself such that when the time comes to 'cast your whole vote,' you're reasonably confident you're not being either fear-based or ego-driven in your choice . . . that the journey you're on is really yours, and not someone else's? If you think of your first few jobs after Yale in this way— holistically and in terms of your growth as a person rather than as ladder rungs to a specific material outcome—you're less likely to wake up at age forty-five married to a stranger."

Yikes!

Professor Charles Hill also believes it's an unproductive use of Yalies' time—but for slightly different reasons. He sees the job world as split into two categories: primary functions and secondary functions, productive and unproductive. Unlike straight-up corporations, he doesn't see these banks or consulting agencies as contributing to the world in a primary, meaningful way.

"People go into it without knowing why," he said. "They consider you a crop. They harvest you, put you in their grinder, pay you well, and off-load you." He sees consulting services as something companies invest in to protect against potential lawsuits—providing somewhere for CEOs to point the finger in the event of legal trouble. When the economy goes down, corporations cut back on the use of consultants. Hill argues that if their services were truly needed, the exact opposite would occur (i.e., the corporate use of consultants would increase).

His alternative? Professor Hill wishes more Yalies would go into the productive economy, i.e., work for the corporations themselves.

"Students have these ideologies dropped down on them from the sixties and seventies about corporations being evil," he said. "For some reason people will work for consultants and banks but not for PepsiCo or General Motors." As for the nonprofit world, Hill sees it as a waste of our talents. "It's a question of grand strategy," he said, insisting that our energy is better spent elsewhere.

Yikes!

As far as *other important people* go, university president Richard Levin believes "there are many ways to contribute to the well-being of society, and there are many forms of public service." He rejects the notion that "people who choose a business career aren't interested in being public-spirited," asserting that "what's outstanding about Yale graduates is that whatever career they choose, they end up being active participants in the civic life of the communities in which they live."

Harold Bloom disagrees.

"Alas," he groaned, "this is the death of the mind. That is not my vision of Yale University."

* * *

Inevitably, some of the students I spoke with aren't interested in the industry at all. "I can never say for an individual person because I don't know their financial circumstances," Alexandra Brodsky '12 said, "but twenty-five percent is a lot of talent that could do a hell of a lot for the world elsewhere. I think that we have to be aware of that when we make these choices." Brodsky, the co-coordinator of Dwight Hall,* spends a lot of her time at Yale surrounded by nonprofit management. For her, the argument that working in the private sector is the best way to prepare oneself for this line of work is faulty.

"I think the best way to get the skills to work for a nonprofit is to work for a nonprofit," she said. "The answer people give about skills acquisition is very convenient."

Sam Schoenburg '12, a political activist and campaigner, is on the same page. "I've always been interested in government work or advocacy and I don't feel that [consulting or finance] would satisfy me in the same way—even if it was only for a couple of years," he said.

"There seems to be a great disconnect between the lofty

---

* Yale's undergraduate public service organization.

speeches we hear at commencement from Yale administrators about devoting ourselves to public service and the career advice we're presented with during the rest of the year."

Still, some people I talked to were interested in the industry for its own sake—fascinated and excited by the work itself. Three such students requested to remain anonymous, but one, Sam Bekenstein '12, was willing to comment on his genuine interest in consulting as a career choice in itself, not as a means to another end.

"In my everyday decision making, I want to be doing something that has an impact," he said, "and when I think about how best to be in that position, I usually think of some kind of strategic management."

Joe Breen '12 is caught somewhere in the middle. He's interested in eventually going into affordable housing development, running a nonprofit that improves services for a community or provides services that do not yet exist. But he's applying for a series of jobs in the real estate private sector and isn't sure how he feels about it morally.

"It's hard to say which types of things are improving communities and which are exploiting communities," he said. "But ultimately, I want to work for an organization that I'm positive is not exploiting communities for profit."

Joe isn't sure where commercial real estate falls on that spectrum, and it frustrates him.

"I would love for there to be a great two-year program that helps you gain all of these skills and gets you to start helping people right away, but I haven't found that yet," he said. "It's pretty hard to be proactive in finding your own alternative, meaningful experience when you're running an organization and taking classes. These commercial systems are already in place. They have deadlines. They present themselves to you."

At times, Breen admits, he worries we're sending our "best and brightest" into jobs that "abuse communities for profit." (He also worries that every quote he gave for this article has the word *community* in it.)

The Office of Yale Undergraduate Career Services is well aware of these complaints. But Associate Dean and UCS Director Allyson Moore contends that they're seeking to answer them.

"We recognize that financial services and management consulting firms have a wealth of resources at their disposal and that their on-campus recruiting efforts are thus highly visible," she said via e-mail. "That means there is a responsibility for UCS to help those industries with fewer resources, such as arts, nonprofit, and public sectors, to receive equal visibility." This year, they made sure that one third of the organizations at the career fair were from these categories.

"We were quite pleased with that," she said, "and will continue these efforts within the coming months." One such initiative is an online self-assessment service designed to identify students' passions so they can "hone in on motivations" to better address their needs.

* * *

Honestly, I think UCS is an easy scapegoat. The real reason so many of us pursue careers in consulting and finance is far more complicated than that. Of course, the word *scapegoat* is problematic to begin with. Are consulting firms inherently evil? Probably not. Are banks inherently evil? Probably not. Frankly, I don't know enough about *everything* to make a statement like that one way or another. So is there anything intrinsically wrong with the fact that 25 percent of employed Yale graduates end up in this industry?

Yeah. I think so.

Of course this is my own opinion, but to me there's something sad about so many of us entering a line of work in which we're not (for the most part) producing something, or helping someone, or engaging in something that we're explicitly passionate about. Even if it's just for two or three years. That's a lot of years! And these aren't just years. This is twenty-three and twenty-four and twenty-five. If it were a smaller percentage of people, perhaps it wouldn't bother me so much. But it's not.

What it boils down to is that we could be doing other things. Sure, working at Bain or McKinsey or J.P. Morgan might be one way to gain skills to help us get hired elsewhere, but it's obviously not the only option. There's a lot of cool shit we could all be doing—and I don't need to enumerate the clichés.

Obviously, some people need to make money. They have school loans to pay off and families to support. For those of us with an actual need to make money quickly, these industries might make a lot of sense. In fact, I think that working hard to earn a decent amount of money can be quite noble. I'm still struggling with the fact that due to my own (selfish) desire to be a writer, my children probably won't have the same opportunities I had growing up. For most students, however, I genuinely don't think it's about the money. It's a factor, sure. But it just feels like a factor.

What bothers me is this idea of validation, of rationalization. The notion that some of us (regardless of what we tell ourselves) are doing this because we're not sure what else to do and it's easy to apply to and it will pay us decently and it will make us feel like we're still successful. I just haven't met that many people who sound genuinely excited about these jobs. That's super depressing! I don't understand why no one is talking about it.

Oftentimes at Yale, I'll be sitting around studying or drinking or hanging out when I'll hear one of my friends talk about a project they're doing for a class or a rally they're organizing or a play they're putting on. And I'll just think, really, honestly, how remarkably privileged we are to hang around with such a talented group of people around here. I am constantly reminded of the immense passion and creativity of those with whom I get to spend time every day.

Maybe I'm overreacting. Maybe it really is a fantastic way to gain valuable, real-world skills. And maybe everyone will quit these jobs in a few years and do something else.

But it worries me.

I want to watch Shloe's movies and I want to see Mark's musicals and I want to volunteer with Joe's nonprofit and eat at Annie's restaurant and send my kids to schools Jeff has reformed and I'm *just scared* about this industry that's taking all my friends and telling them this is the best way for them to be spending their time. Any of their time. Maybe I'm ignorant and idealistic but I just feel like that can't possibly be true. I feel like we know that. I feel like we can do something really cool to this world. And I fear—at twenty-three, twenty-four, twenty-five—we might forget.

The Art of Observation

The old couple in lower berths C and D stared at us for at least twenty of the thirty-two hours between the City of the Dead and India's south coast. We read books, rolled dice, and looked out at rice fields and rivers. The woman was plump and wrapped in a saffron sari, the man thin and clothed in a starched white shirt. We traveled with them in a curtained compartment as the train wove past scruffy monkeys and starving cows, but they gazed instead at our pale peculiarities. The way I braided my hair. The way he bit at a nail. The way we smiled and laughed across our top bunks. We didn't mind, really. Not when they watched us eat oily lentils with forks and not when they spoke in hushed Hindi as we took off our shoes. So we looked out and not down as Calcutta wound to Chennai and the monsoon heat broke: five weeks in and we were used to being watched.

When Luke and I landed in India, we discovered our celebrity before our passports were stamped. Our backpacks rolled through baggage claim and a middle-aged man held out his cell phone and clicked. At first, the attention was surprising. I'd been warned by blogs and travel guides, but I didn't expect such explicit persistence. "One photo, one photo," they'd coo from streets and stands: "One photo, please, miss, one

photo." On our first day in Delhi, the circles in the Jama Mas-
jid mosque forced us off its hot marble and our trip to the
spice bazaar yielded three or four photos. Thrust into a city
where chaos prevails, we were dizzied into frame after frame
with beaming locals. We'd agree to one shot and be trapped in
five others, avoid followers at lunch only to get them at dinner. By the time we'd traveled west into the desert, Luke was
getting fed up. He'd refuse cameras and yell off those who
stared, exhausted and appalled by the endless annoyance.

I liked it.

When a rickshaw driver turned around or a schoolboy
held out his phone, I flattered myself beyond the obvious
parameters. I knew, of course, that my white skin and light
features were responsible for the attention, but some part of
me still took pleasure from being stared at on trains and photographed in city gardens. I didn't quite mind posing for all
the pictures and felt, rather disgustingly, like some kind of
movie star, forced to pause for snapshots outside shops and
on the streets.

The sentiment sickened me. Each time I felt a twang of
pleasure from the stares or picture requests, my ego was
kicked down by my very revulsion that it had been boosted
in the first place. I pondered my own narcissism as I smiled
again and again next to Taj Mahal tourists from Hyderabad
and Mumbai. "One photo please," they'd ask, and I wouldn't
know how to say no. Luke would walk ahead and I'd inevitably stay behind. If it made them happy, after all, why not play
along?

I confessed such sentiments to two Irish girls on the roof-
top restaurant of a cheap hostel in Jaipur. We complained
about the stares on trains and in rickshaws, comparing stories of extremes as the sun set and kites flew up from the

pink city's nearby roofs. After a few glasses of Indian wine, I offered that maybe, sometimes, it really wasn't so bad. Yes, they responded, nodding and thinking. They agreed with the emotion, they saw what I meant. I laughed at our deprecation as the light faded, but searched their eyes in earnest nonetheless.

Yet as the weeks wore on, it became harder to see fascination as flattery. In the Buddhist town of Dharamsala, Tibetan monks pulled cheap cell phones from within their thick maroon robes and asked grinningly for pictures against the Himalayan skyline. In a rural village near Jaisalmer, a man had me pose with each of his skinny children. In the City of the Dead, no cameras were allowed. The dying come to die in the holy Ganges River, burning on its banks and escaping reincarnation in its waters. Walking through the chaos of bells, human ashes, stray dogs, and bones, I felt a kind of double relief. Not a single Indian requested a photograph, and not one time did I snap my own lens. One night during the monsoon, we wandered down the shore to watch the cremations, standing beside bald men as they threw powders into fires that raged despite the rain. Not a single person was looking at us.

The next morning we boarded a thirty-two-hour train. In the afternoon, Luke climbed down off his berth, past the thin aged man and his saffron wife, wandering out between the cars to see the jungle fade to palms. I opened my journal to begin writing and caught the corners of my eyes watching the woman watch me. My prose was jumbled and distracted and I was reminded for an instant of a performance-art piece at the Public Theater. An actress worked on a typewriter in a corner of the lobby—claiming art through the action of everyday observation. I'd left the theater with an almost angry indignation. There was nothing to be fascinated by, nothing to esteem, nothing to romanticize in this everyday examination of our immutable solipsism.

That night, when the train was dark, the woman's eyes smiled up at me before she faded off to sleep. I heard the rain break and the men vending dosa and chai slowly fade from the aisles. Far from my months stumbling through markets and holy land, I wonder how many photographs of my pale limbs line the walls of strange Indian homes. Embarrassed, I fumbled off my flash from within the stained train sheets, capturing the woman to bring home to a tiny box on my shelf.

Song for the Special

Every generation thinks it's special—my grandparents because they remember World War II, my parents because of discos and the moon. We have the Internet. Millions and billions of doors we can open and shut, posting ourselves into profiles and digital scrapbooks. Suddenly and totally, we're threaded together in a network so terrifyingly colossal that we can finally see our terrifyingly tiny place in it. But we're all individuals. It's beaten into us in MLK Day assemblies (one person can make a difference!) and fourth-grade poster projects (what do you want to be when you grow up?). We can be anything! Our parents are divorced but we're in love! Vaguely, quietly, we know we'll be famous. For being president, for starring in a movie, for writing a feature at eighteen in the *New York Times*.

I'm so jealous. Unthinkable jealousies, jealousies of the Pulitzer Prize–winning novel I'm reading and the Oscar-winning movie I just saw. Why didn't I think to rewrite *Mrs. Dalloway*? I should have thought to chronicle a schizophrenic ballerina. It's inexcusable. Everyone else is so successful, and I hate them. There's a German word I learned about in psychology class called *schadenfreude*, which means a pleasure derived from the misfortune of others. The word flips into my head like a shaming pop-up when a girl doesn't get the internship either or a boy's show is bad. I was lying in bed the other night wondering whether the Germans created a word for its opposite when I realized that the displeasure derived from the fortune of others is easier to spell. I should have thought to coin its green eyes.

I blame the Internet. Its inconsiderate inclusion of everything. Success is transparent and accessible, hanging down where it can tease but not touch us. We talk into these scratchy microphones and take extra photographs but I still feel like there are just SO MANY PEOPLE. Every day, 1,035.6 books are published; sixty-six million people update their status each morning. At night, aimlessly scrolling, I remind myself of elementary school murals. One person can make a difference! But the people asking me what I want to be when I grow up don't want me to make a poster anymore. They want me to fill out forms and hand them rectangular cards that say HELLO THIS IS WHAT I DO.

I went to an arts conference in Manhattan last spring and everyone was scrambling to meet everyone, asserting their individuality like sad salesmen. This is my idea, I would say, this is my thing. We stood in cocktail circles and exchanged earnest interest. Hoo, hoo! Open spaces! Ohh yes! The avant garde! I didn't have a business card. It didn't even occur to me. It might have been funny or endearing but I ended up just being embarrassed. I don't have one, I'd say again and again. (Ha Ha!) Then I'd sit down for another panel to take notes and nod. There were so many people there. There are just so many people.

The thing is, someday the sun is going to die and everything on Earth will freeze. This will happen. Even if we end global warming and clean up our radiation. The complete works of

William Shakespeare, Monet's lilies, all of Hemingway, all of Milton, all of Keats, our music libraries, our library libraries, our galleries, our poetry, our letters, our names etched in desks. I used to think printing things made them permanent, but that seems so silly now. Everything will be destroyed no matter how hard we work to create it. The idea terrifies me. I want tiny permanents. I want gigantic permanents! I want what I think and who I am captured in an anthology of indulgence I can comfortingly tuck into a shelf in some labyrinthine library.

Everyone thinks they're special—my grandma for her Marlboro commercials, my parents for discos and the moon. You can be anything, they tell us. No one else is quite like you. But I searched my name on Facebook and got eight tiny pictures staring back. The Marina Keegans with their little hometowns and relationship statuses. When we die, our gravestones will match. HERE LIES MARINA KEEGAN, they will say. Numbers one, two, three, four, five, six, seven, eight.

I'm so jealous. Laughable jealousies, jealousies of everyone who might get a chance to speak from the dead. I've zoomed out my timeline to include the apocalypse, and, religionless, I worship the potential for my own tangible trace. How presumptuous! To assume specialness in the first place. As I age, I can see the possibilities fade from the fourth-grade displays: it's too late to be a doctor, to star in a movie, to run for president. There's a really good chance I'll never do anything. It's selfish and self-centered to consider, but it scares me.

Sometimes I think about what it would be like if there was actually peace. The whole planet would be super sustainable: windmills everywhere, solar-paneled do-bops, clean streets. Before the world freezes and goes dark, it would be perfect. The generation flying its tiny cars would think itself special.

Until one day, vaguely, quietly, the sun would flicker out and they'd realize that none of us are. Or that all of us are.

I read somewhere that radio waves just keep traveling outward, flying into the universe with eternal vibrations. Sometime before I die I think I'll find a microphone and climb to the top of a radio tower. I'll take a deep breath and close my eyes because it will start to rain right when I reach the top. Hello, I'll say to outer space, this is my card.

About the Author

Marina Keegan (1989–2012) was an award-winning author, journalist, playwright, poet, actress, and activist. Her nonfiction has been published in the *New York Times*; her fiction has been published on NewYorker.com and read on NPR's *Selected Shorts*; her musical, *Independents*, was a *New York Times* Critics' Pick. Marina's final essay for the *Yale Daily News*, "The Opposite of Loneliness," became an instant global sensation, viewed by more than 1.4 million people from ninety-eight countries. For more information, please visit www.theoppositeofloneliness.com.

A Remembrance of Marina Keegan and Questions for Further Discussion

Though Marina Keegan wrote most of the pieces included in *The Opposite of Loneliness* when she was a student at Yale, as one of her high school English teachers, I first knew her at the Buckingham Browne & Nichols School in Cambridge, Massachusetts. She played on my soccer team her freshman fall, filled my sophomore class with a swirl of impish energy and adult insight, and then took (and often led) my senior fall elective. Once she headed off to college, she regularly returned to visit several of her former teachers, surging into our offices with updates, stories, schemes, and ambitions, yet also questions about us, about our lives. Marina and I kept running into each other unexpectedly, too—at Fenway Park or in Harvard Square or on the summer evening when I spotted her distinctive car gliding alongside me on I-93 South in New Hampshire, so we pulled over at the next exit to catch up. We assigned each other books to read: Mark Helprin's *Winter's Tale* came from me, and Neil Gaiman's *American Gods* was her pick one year. She and I e-mailed back and forth, creating a paper trail that I now treasure, particularly for the updates Marina sent after the night she celebrated Obama winning his first term and the day she earned a tableful of approving nods during a Yale seminar by raising a point from *The Great Gatsby* that we had discussed years before.

Marina loved school and flung herself into it. She wondered in her essay "The Opposite of Loneliness," "More than once I've looked back on my high school self and thought: how did I do that? How did I work so hard?" But work she did, tearing through BB&N, inspiring her peers, and combatting complacency in any form. Even when she was still so young, her passions were clear and wide-ranging: Shakespeare, Harry Potter, Democratic causes, Rubik's Cubes, Model United Nations, the theater's power, any good argument, her camp friends, the funny thing that happened as she tried to park when arriving late to school, and on and on.

Those of us lucky enough to have taught Marina will never forget that experience; she was quite simply a force of nature in our classrooms. As Amy Selinger, Marina's history teacher and later her academic advisor, wrote, "Any goal that included channeling the whirlwind that was freshman Marina was pure folly. She tugged, pulled, and pushed all of us to challenge her, forcing me to be a better teacher and demanding that our class look beyond the surface, beyond what was easy. I was exhausted. I was thrilled. I can't remember a Medieval History class ever being so dynamic, engaging, or interesting."

In my own courses, Marina wowed us with her exceptional intellect, irrepressible energy, and mischievous humor, whether we were reading *Macbeth*, "Ode on a Grecian Urn," or *Atonement*. She outthought and outargued everyone in her class as the top sophomore debater even as she brutalized major characters' names with her "creative" spellings on exam essays. Only she could get away with joyfully interrupting the group discussion with the incoming text message (on a cell phone illegally left on) that J. K. Rowling would be Harvard's next commencement speaker, addressing the crowds that would gather just a short walk away from where we sat. I saved a copy of nearly all of Marina's essays; they were simply too good to be returned without keeping a lasting record. In one scene from her final paper, a ten-page emulation of *The English Patient*, the thumbless former thief Caravaggio found doorknobs jeering at him. Michael Ondaatje might easily have confused her prose for his own, and grading it felt simply like reading for pleasure. Given this seemingly endless onslaught of insight and imagination and spunk, my college recommendation for Marina promised, "I will be citing her ideas to future groups of students for years to come," a statement that I did not intend to be proven quite so profoundly true.

From early on, Marina thus set the pace for the wholehearted, full-souled, big-brained commitment to activism, artistry, and academics that carried her so far in her limited years. During her many visits back to school, we talked about what she might do in the future: write, or run for office, or perhaps teach. She knew she wanted to make a difference, and when her father left a job in business to teach middle school social studies, she was both proud and thrilled. Equally important, everyone who met Marina seemed to come away with a story, somehow changed by even the briefest of encounters; her immediacy and vitality had staying power. As a younger BB&N student who looked up to Marina told me, "She turned a lot of people into who they are."

Since the tragedy of Marina's death, her parents have heard from strangers around the globe surprised to find themselves writing to share the impact of "meeting" Marina through her words: Jewish teenagers visiting a series of concentration camps while on "The March of the Living" and finding specific comfort and renewed purpose in her writings; college peers living more mindfully; musicians writing songs inspired by her; older readers making midlife recalibrations and career changes, whether they are returning to school or shifting to a nonprofit or finishing that manuscript; people simply rediscovering a sense of hope. These new life paths all build from Marina's own sense that it's never too late to change, that we must take action, that we are indeed "in this together."

One of the final e-mails I received from Marina included the line "Meanwhile, I just had my last. ever. yale. class. omg." I can *hear* her voice in that typed sentence, just as I can hear how she would have delivered the dialogue in her plays or read aloud from the essays and stories in this collection. Each word that she left behind is precious, including the simple three I rediscovered a few days after Marina's memorial service. Her long-forgotten note, scrawled with a dry-erase marker on the back of a BB&N book slip and left on my desk when she was visiting from college, simply read, "Marina was here!"

Marina was here.

Yes, she was, in so many ways. And with an exclamation point.

My hope is that through this book and Marina's many legacies, we may all still hear her and be inspired by how she used her fleeting time to be passionately, vibrantly, fully here.

—Beth McNamara
August 2014

The following questions are intended for a variety of audiences—the members of a book group, students in a college seminar or upper-level high school class, or individual readers taking time for further reflection. Some questions address the larger motivations behind Marina Keegan's work; some examine technical, structural, or thematic elements within her prose; some consider her legacy as an activist pushing her readers to take action; some focus on the young woman now so dearly missed. Of course, all of these questions serve only as starting points. The best discussions will occur as you take these prompts in the directions that most fascinate, puzzle, or inspire you.

1. Marina Keegan wrote the essay "The Opposite of Loneliness" specifically for her Yale graduation in 2012, and the single line "The hats" refers to the college's Class Day tradition of seniors wearing creative, colorful hats. Yet many readers have found its message to be universal, evoking their own days at college, at camp, or in any other tight-knit community. What makes Keegan's words apply to any group of people who have found a powerful sense of connection? What would you define as your own personal opposite of loneliness?

2. In "The Opposite of Loneliness," Keegan insists, "What we have to remember is that we can still do anything. We can change our minds. We can start over" (p. 3). After reading this piece, have you realized you want to reevaluate anything in your own life? Given her sense of possibility and hope, as well as the permission to fail, is there some goal or project you now feel empowered to pursue?

3. Some reviewers have responded most powerfully to Keegan's nonfiction, while others find the fiction more compelling. Do you prefer the stories or the essays? Does this choice match your usual preference for fiction or nonfiction? Which individual piece has stayed with you most vividly, and why?

4. Several lines from Keegan's poems are quoted between sections of the book, and her spoken-word performances

of the poems "Bygones," "I Don't Know about Art," "Nuclear Spring," and "Rolling Stones" all appear online at theoppositeofloneliness.com. After viewing these short videos, what do you notice in her delivery, and how does this influence your understanding and appreciation of her work? What does she emphasize through her pacing and voice? How does her physical presence affect each piece?

5. Anne Fadiman's introduction offers a powerful set of insights into Marina as a young woman and a writer. How do these shared moments shape your reading of the collection?

6. As Fadiman notes, one of Marina's strengths is that she writes in her own voice as a young person. What about her depiction of young love is particularly evocative? What does young love have that more mature love lacks, and what does mature love offer that is missing in young love?

7. Despite the collection's youthful energy, many readers have also found Keegan's voice to be entirely universal, the offerings of an old soul. What wisdom beyond her years does she share?

8. The cover photo, taken by Joy Shan, Yale class of 2015, captures Marina's direct, confident presence. This image also evokes the sense of fleeting time Keats addresses in "Ode on a Grecian Urn," a poem that in "Cold Pastoral" Claire is taught has "tragedy . . . in eternal stasis" (p. 10). At which moments in the text does Marina's individual voice appear most distinctly, similarly freezing her message in a single moment or idea?

9. "Cold Pastoral" offers a haunting look at how a college community reacts to the sudden death of a young person. What interpersonal dynamics resonate for you as Claire reconsiders her relationship with Brian, her sense of herself, and her unexpected connections to Lauren?

10. Keegan was also a gifted playwright. Within the dialogue that appears in her stories, how does she employ specific rhythms and diction that reflect this background? In terms of pacing, tone, or emphasis, what advice would you give to someone performing these pieces or reading them aloud?

11. Though Keegan was vibrantly alive in person, her writing often considers death and mortality. One of the adult characters in her play *Utility Monster* says, "I wanted to do something important . . . I wanted to contribute *something* that would be there when I wasn't." Once you know that Keegan died in a car accident just five days after she graduated from college, what lines from her stories and essays strike you most powerfully?

12. In her personal journal, Keegan wrote, "I hate that I feel I am running out of time. I must always remember that time is all there is and we are always running out of it." At what points in this collection do you feel a similar sense of urgency? Is living with an appreciation of time's swift passage ultimately empowering or limiting?

13. Keegan's stories and characters employ many light moments and quick one-liners. When does her humor emerge to shift the tone or underline her message? What moments made you laugh out loud?

14. The inability to see is central to both "Reading Aloud" and "Challenger Deep," while the narrator in "The Art of Observation" initially relishes being looked at and photographed before she flips roles and snaps a picture of the woman who had been watching her. How does Keegan's writing make use of the senses—both visual and nonvisual—to make the reader's experience more powerful? In addition to these examples of physical blindness, which stories include characters metaphorically blind to what lies before them?

15. Specific mentions of Keats, *Swan Lake*, Andy Warhol, Salvador Dalí, *Othello*, Islamic architecture, Shakespeare, Monet's lilies, Hemingway, Milton, and libraries appear throughout this collection. How do these scholarly and artistic references enhance the more informal tone of Keegan's prose?

16. The last paragraphs of individual stories are worth careful examination and rereading. What details does Keegan set up earlier in each piece to make these endings particularly powerful? How does she seal each story while still using a light hand? When does she allow ambiguity? Which ending do you see as most effective, and why?

17. "Stability in Motion" uses the evolution of Keegan's car to parallel her own journey during those years. What individual details make the story most vivid? What imagery, such as the deconstructed scrapbook (p. 148), is most evocative in describing this time? Do you have an object or place in your own life that tracks a similar sense of growth or change?

18. Any skilled writer focuses not only on individual sentences and images but also the larger structure of her work. In "Why We Care about Whales," look for how Keegan manages the transitions between evocative descriptions, scientific research, individual experiences, whale-based crises, human suffering, a specific call to action, and the narrative of the dying whale. Young writers might even color-code the individual "modes" to see when, how, and why Keegan shifts her focus. Another way to examine a writer's internal structure is to physically cut up a copy of a piece and then try to reassemble the individual paragraphs in the original order; try this with "I Kill for Money."

19. "Against the Grain" is particularly poignant and personal as it captures the voice of an exasperated teenager who comes to appreciate the lengths to which a parent will go to care for her child. What details are most effective in shaping these shifts in voice, and how does Keegan craft the moments of final realization? What is the effect of the story's non-chronological sequencing and splicing of scenes? In a broader sense, when can well-intentioned parenting meant to protect or support actually result in harm?

20. The day she graduated from college, Keegan told her mother that she was especially proud of her *Yale Daily News* article "Even Artichokes Have Doubts," which went on to be adapted for the *New York Times* and discussed on NPR. When *The Opposite of Loneliness* was first published in April 2014, columnist Nicholas Kristof wrote, "Keegan was right to prod us all to reflect on what we seek from life, to ask these questions, to recognize the importance of passions

as well as paychecks—even if there are no easy answers." As Keegan reminds other young people that "we can do something really cool to this world" (p. 200), what points does she emphasize? What counterarguments might she have considered more specifically? Do you share her concern about where so many top young graduates take their first jobs? Do you worry that you need to compromise your own dreams for practical concerns? Why or why not?

21. Keegan often mentions jealousy, either in romantic triangles such as those depicted in "Cold Pastoral" and "The Ingenue" or as she considers others achieving success (p. 205). Ironically, she even mentions "jealousies of everyone who might get a chance to speak from the dead" (p. 207). How does this very human admission affect your attitude toward her work? What do her jealousy and the confessed objects of her jealousy reveal?

22. In pieces like "Why We Care about Whales," "Putting the 'Fun' Back in Eschatology," and "Song for the Special," Keegan shares her concerns for the planet and the entire human race. She admits, "I worry sometimes that humans are afraid of helping humans" (p. 153), even as she remembers the elementary school insistence that "One person can make a difference" (p. 206). She notes that "Fifty stranded whales are a tangible crisis with a visible solution" (p. 154), while climate change, homelessness, hunger, and other national or global issues seem entirely intractable. In your view, is she right? What stands in our way of truly making this a better world? Why don't we realize that "we're in this together"? Why does Keegan still find hope in humanity?

23. Look back across the entire collection to see how Keegan's titles stand out for their specificity, individuality, and punch. Which title is the most striking or initially the most unexpected? What larger patterns stand out in what she chooses to emphasize? Which title most affected your understanding of the piece that followed, and why?

24. "The Opposite of Loneliness" and "Even Artichokes Have Doubts" have clear activist messages, and Yale professors Anne Fadiman and Harold Bloom note that Keegan is working against "the death of literature" (p. xi) and "the death of the mind" (p. 196). In her poem "I Don't Know about Art," she wonders if "my play, my poem, my song, will make a difference. / Or it won't." Given that "Song for the Special" ends with Keegan offering her card to the universe, how do you describe her impact or define her legacy?

For an extended reading guide featuring further questions for discussion, please visit theoppositeofloneliness.com.